TOBA

At the Hands of a Thief

TOBA
At the Hands of a Thief

MICHAEL MARK

Bradbury Press · New York

Bradbury Press
An Affiliate of Macmillan, Inc.
866 Third Avenue, New York, N.Y. 10022
Collier Macmillan Canada, Inc.
Manufactured in the United States of America
10 9 8 7 6 5 4 3 2 1
The text of this book is set in 12 pt. Garamond.

Library of Congress Cataloging in Publication Data:
Mark, Michael, 1957– Toba at the hands of a thief.
Summary: Presents eleven episodes from the life of a Polish teenager as she prepares to leave her Jewish family for a new life in America during the early 1900's.
[1. Jews—Poland—Fiction 2. Poland—Fiction] I. Title.
PZ7.M33927Tob 1985 [Fic] 84-20456
ISBN 0-02-762310-6

For the real characters in my life—
my Mom, Dad, brother and bear

The New World

The moon makes its nightly journey over the near hills of Lenchintz, over clouds dark with promise of needed rain, over a still Toba, lost in wonder that this same moon shines on the land of America, the place they call the New World.

What is it about this country? Is it not made of earth and rocks, does it not sprout trees with fruit to eat—this land hushed as if holy? *America*.

Toba envisions an evil woman behind a kindly face and humble features, who offers strangers tempting meals with delicate aromas that disguise the poison spices.

Many have been fooled at this witch's table. They take

her smooth hand and follow her to an enormous feast. But one bite, one swallow, and the spell is forever cast, the eater forever changed, forever lost.

All her life, Toba has heard and read stories of the wandering Jews—how they were forced from their homes, fleeing enemies, searching for a place of peace. But these are old stories of days long gone, faded with age—or so Toba had thought until Jenny, her closest friend, and her family announced their plans to leave Lenchintz—where Jenny was born, where her sisters, brother and momma and papa were born—to find a new home across the deep waters, in a place they had never seen, where the language is strange and the ways unknown.

"We are leaving," announced Jenny's papa, waving his pipe before his freshly shaven face, "because America offers our children a future."

There was a great commotion. Shouts of joy, waves of tears, warnings, promises, debates loud and furious. But three days later, everything became quiet. All that was left of Jenny and Toba's friendship was a silk blouse. The one Toba had always admired. Jenny had wrapped the present in new paper; on it she had written an oath. *This ship may carry away my body, but I will leave my soul with you, in Poland.* She also swore she would *write long letters of this America and her false dreams.*

Jenny's body was taken by that ship nearly two years ago, but not one letter has arrived proving America a liar, and Toba feels certain that her old friend's soul must somehow have stolen aboard, also never to return.

"Yes," Toba tells herself and the watchful moon. "The witch's poison forces the promises from your head and turns your back on the people you love."

Jenny's family were not the only ones to turn from their homes. Whole towns, as if taken by the plague, have in the dark of night packed their few belongings and fled, leaving their homes, friends, families, hollowed, abandoned. This plague has struck the young as well as the old, separated lovers, severed children from the arms of their grieved parents; families have been torn apart, leaving behind countless souls, to be talked of, hoped for, mourned.

Toba picks at the envelope she has been carrying with her since early this morning—writings from the pen of one of the lost souls. The envelope arrived with its edges chewed and half-opened from its travels, but the letter it holds has been folded and bent in every corner by Toba's searching hands, as if she has tried squeezing every drop of meaning, every feeling, from the small ink marks.

Slowly, half afraid, half curious—as if she hasn't already memorized each word of each paragraph, or she hopes the letters will somehow have moved about and rearranged their message—Toba pulls out the letter, unfolds and smooths the worn pages. She turns to catch the moon's weak light.

12 April 1915
New York City. America

My dearest sister,

I know these words will find you healthy and enjoying Lenchintz's most beautiful season. It's only seven months that I am gone, but already Poland seems like a place I have dreamed, a world that filled my head one night of restless sleep.

Toba forces her eyes from the words.

Only seven months and what had been her life is now a dream! Soon, three months—less!—what is her sister's family will become strangers who only visit in her sleep. Faceless people, with unfamiliar names, people who will fade from her memory to be forgotten.

"*America!*"

Let me tell you of my days, my season in New York City. You already know I have fled from my old room in Mrs. Ketchum's boarding house, where they robbed me for eight dollars a week for a room the size of a pill box. Now I live with Mrs. Levenstein's family—a friend of Momma's from Lodz. For six dollars, I have a larger room, though if it had a window I would not complain. There are eight of us. A tiny Poland in a single house.

How strange! America is so large, yet we are forced into such crowded corners. But this is not forever.

Every night, after work, while dinner is being prepared, we sit and try to improve our English, this crazy language with evil tricks waiting to trip our tongues, but before too long we are back to speaking the easy flow of our Yiddish. It is just as well. After ten hours of work, our mouths are only good for eating Mrs. Levenstein's steamy meals.

After dinner, we sit and listen to the news and programs on the radio. A great deal we do not understand. Soon we fall to our beds to sleep, to dream of our bright futures, of speaking perfect English, dressing in styled, expensive clothes, having our families near. Only a moment passes before we are woken, still tired, to return to our work and listen to the pounding of new buildings being born. Metal against metal—this is the music of the New World.

"Noise! Noise from machines—this is *music*!" There is no question, only disgust in Toba's voice. "This is the person who would hum and sing for days until the whole family would either stuff their ears with cotton or join in? This is what soothes her at night? This is what America has done—deafened her so she cannot tell the difference between noise and song!"

Oh, but Toba, believe me, there is truly no more wonderful sound in any language than *America*. Here, every day is freshly born! We are children. "Greenhorns," they call us. When we say a word that does not fit, or answer, "How are you today?" with, "Yes, I would like a piece of fish," they laugh and say we are "Right off the boat." We are "green." This means we are new, unrippened Americans. But what has more promise than unripe fruit—tell me that, Tobala! We pick an apple from a branch, breathe its hard scent, pinch its thick skin, and we know that this fruit has not yet fulfilled its journey—but wait! Soon, soon the apple will turn color, it will become fragrant and soft to the touch, telling us how sweet it will taste, wet with juice and tender meat. We will be fulfilled! This is us, Toba, my peach. This is you and me, here, in the garden of America.

"Peach! Apple!" Toba muses, knowing the truth behind these tempting, empty words. They are, she is sure, the very words Eve spoke to Adam, not in the garden of America, but in Eden. She reads aloud, her voice sharp with mistrust. " 'We will be fulfilled!' The words of a serpent."

How you looked at me the morning I left. I will never forget your eyes, burning like two coals.

But take those eyes and look at what America has already done. Momma has written of Papa's good fortune with his new scarves. They are selling more easily since he is using the better material. But such fabric is costly. I am no messiah, I know. But still, if I had not come to America, where would the money have come from to buy such cloth?

Toba, you must understand that you are not a child any longer. Your gift is your youth, but such flames die. Here, you will breathe the free air of possibility. An education you will have from the finest scholars. You will be the painter you have always wanted to be.

"I have not painted in years," Toba accuses, mourns.

And what you will see! If only I could open a window from Lenchintz to New York City, you would marvel at the boulevards crowded with every type of person, selling what your eyes will not allow you to believe. Street carts piled with clothing more beautiful than you can imagine. Fruits and vegetables spill into sacks as if from invisible trees. Automobiles without horses move along, carrying gentlemen. Everything! If America means only one word, it is *everything*.

"*Nothing*," Toba the snake hisses. "America is *nothing*."

All I ask is that you take the money I have sent and buy a ticket on what Mrs. Levenstein calls the Life Boat. Come, Toba, come to me.

I must close my eyes and rest now. Please do not be angry with me. I cannot bear to think of you standing so still, your hands clenched, your eyes burning—as is your unforgivable habit.

Toba, come to me.

Bella

It is a few moments before Toba's sister's determined voice fades. Carefully fitting the limp letter into its wrinkled envelope, Toba notices how dark the night has become. The moon is hiding behind the low clouds. Even the air is black. It is a blackness Toba can feel.

First the light of Anna's room was dimmed when she married Benjamin. Then Bella's room was stilled.

Toba tries to imagine her room without her. It is an impossible thought. Once this house seemed so small, crowded with busy life, loud with voices, and hungry eaters. But no longer. They have been chased away, have followed each other, have taken their bodies and left their souls, which feed off the shadows.

"She has been poisoned," Toba hisses, clutching the letter unmercifully, ignoring the thin voice in her head telling her that she is being too hard on her sister.

"*English. Buildings. Automobiles*," Toba lists, turning angrily back to the house. "These are things to take the place of the country where you were *born*? A family who has given you all they have? Work all day and sleep to wake tired! This is a life to run to? This is what she wants for *me*?"

The only response to Toba's questions is the distant rumble of thunder. A drop of rain falls against her cheek. She wonders if it ever rains in this perfect New World, if anyone cries—or is this against their laws? Perhaps they send you back to Poland if you cry in *America*!

"I will not go to such a place!" Toba shouts, her fist choking the letter, warning the spying eye of the moon.

Again, she is answered with faint thunder, though closer, and another kiss of rain.

When Bella left, Toba had refused her a goodbye kiss. She'd refused Bella her blessing, though Momma and Papa had given theirs. Toba had held fast to her distaste for America and her unwillingness to let Bella be another soulless body to wander away.

But somewhere Toba did offer a silent wish for Bella's health and good fortune in such a wonderous place. She scolded herself for such weakness. But it is true, she must admit, this witch does have a soft, caring face, doesn't she? And her meal's aroma is certainly tempting. Toba can imagine all Bella must see each day. A circus with each sunrise. The way she describes this America in her letters, it is almost too fantastic, too much like one of those dreams after a supper of spicy cabbage and beef. But Bella is not the only one to write such words, paint such visions; others have written of this huge land, overflowing with sparkling and powerful gifts. Places with names like California, Boston, Maryland, Bronx. These names, so foreign-sounding, whisper in Toba's ear, find their way to her tongue and there tickle her like the limericks she has recited in school. And with each, Toba's mind flies off in uncharted directions, sometimes for hours without even a familiar cloud to get in her way.

Cleveland, where Jenny's family brought her, carries to Toba high rivers of wheat, stretching to a sun as gold as women's jewelry, and little barns—the size of wood carvings—housing powerful horses, gentle cows and sleeping sheep.

Bronx, a city inside the New York City, is crowded with quick-tongued salesmen flashing smiles and silver coins, women who wear grand dresses that catch the wind to show their tiny feet. Great buildings stand shoulder to shoulder, straight and proud as soldiers.

Maryland is all white: the homes, trees, streets, even the earth. And very quiet. People talk in whispers, if they speak at all, as they pass each other in their peaceful town. The fruits on the trees and bushes burst from their stems into the mouths of well-mannered children.

Even when she is unwilling, Toba has slipped off to visit such places.

But just as mysteriously as their names give flight to her imagination, she will suddenly be forced to the ground. A familiar scent will sting her nose, a voice calls her name, she will find herself in the middle of a chore—all bringing her back, pulling hard, forcing her two feet to firmly root.

Now Toba stands before her large, dark house, knowing well where she is. She hears deep claps of thunder over her head, and watches the same moon she has always known swim about the dark clouds like a hungry fish nibbling at the stars. The rain will be good, Toba thinks. It will wash all this cloudiness from her head, relieve this heavy feeling of doubt which has weighed her down for too long. Maybe she will let the rain soak her through. She will stand right here, under Poland's sky, on Poland's land, and prove how much she cares for her home.

A cannon of thunder fires.

"Toba!"

She looks up to the black sky. Thunder again carries her name.

"Toba!"

She waits for the answer to her only question. But the thunder does not return. The voice is silent. There is only the wind rustling the leaves, and the birds chirping nervously.

Finally Toba can bear it no longer.

"Should I go to the New World?" she cries.

"Yes, my darling." The voice does not sound in thunder. It is near and calm. A voice Toba loves and could not bear to leave. "You go to this New World."

Toba looks to the dark room of the house. Her Papa's workroom. Now they are both blind; their eyes cannot guide them.

Thunder opens the sky and lets fall a heavy rain.

"Come now, Toba."

Only Toba's heart moves, keeping pace with the million tiny fingers stroking her.

The ocean which Toba refuses to cross is now coming to claim her, filling the ground like Noah's great flood, to carry her off.

"Come, Toba. Come now!"

Toba is not sure whether she is being called from the house, so near, or from as far away as New York City, America.

The letter in her hand grows limp and heavy with water, but Toba holds firm, as if it were the only piece of land to cling to in a great sea.

"Toba, come. Come to me."

She is unable to see her Papa who is so close, but in her mind she can see Bella standing on the shore of a gleaming America, smiling, ghostly. She feels herself drifting, as if the winds are about to sweep her away with the flood. She is drifting backward, away. Farther from her empty house, from Poland, drifting away even from herself.

"Toba!" The name is hushed in her ear.

The drifting stops. A strong current takes her by the arm. She is led up three stairs out of the rain, into the doorway, saving her, Toba feels, from being carried away and drowned.

Carefully, thoroughly, she is towel-dried by busy hands. The stubborn silence that has settled and refuses to lift tells Toba this is forever. "Metal against metal," she remembers. "The music of the New World."

Her Papa sits in his chair at the table. He has said nothing since pointing to Toba's future. Momma only grunts and sighs, working on Toba's face and neck. "Yes, my darling. You will go . . ." It seems to Toba that she is being cleaned, polished, being made perfect for the last time. As if America were one big stage which she must walk across, be presented upon, all shining new. All the warnings—not to run down the stairs, not to speak with a mouth full of food, not to yell across the room, not to lie or be unkind—have all been for this one occasion, all spoken, lectured, repeated, for this one purpose.

America.

When she is dry and there is nothing left of the letter in her hand but the ink stains which have cried their story all over the page, Toba quietly walks up the stairs.

She comes to Anna's room, where she has not been in months, opens the door and lights the lantern still on the old table. In Bella's room, a room Toba swore she'd never enter again, she does the same. And in her own room she lets the flame grow high and wild.

Now all the lost souls can see this house, glowing like a candle in the dark. Jenny, Bella and all the nameless others can see this is where Toba lives.

Closing her eyes, Toba sees herself walking out of her room, down the stairs, out the front door. She turns to look back at the one house in Lenchintz, in all of Poland, that is so bright on this storming night. In the silence, she hears the loud and living voices of her past rise up and carry her away.

The Song of Work

After she finishes mopping the kitchen floor, Toba will climb the stairs to dust the furniture, piece by piece. "And not just around, but beneath and between, too," was Momma's pointed reminder. This will be followed by sweeping the stairs and polishing the banister—and she must not forget the chest of drawers in Papa's workroom waiting to be oiled. The summer's heat has dried and cracked the smooth pine like years on an old face.

It is early yet. Momma is at the market, though perhaps, Toba thinks, she has not yet arrived. It is quite possible she has met another shopper on the way and they have slowed their pace to allow for a decent talk. Papa is in shul praying—deep in a conversation begun years and years ago. The birds are beginning to speak as well, though weakly, morning quiet in their voices. They search for the tune of the day while the sun struggles to rise and push off its milky blanket of last night's clouds and dreams.

Toba, most likely, will not have much chance to be outside on what promises to be a cheerful, lazy day. This, she must admit, is mostly her own fault. She could have taken care of the chores earlier, one at a time. The dusting one morning—a good time for such a job, the light always playful with the fine specks. She could have decided to wash the kitchen floor on a dry afternoon, which would have saved her from mopping. And oiling the furniture, a process which is boring, painful and the most dreaded of all, could have been accomplished a little each day. She could have done all this, but it always seemed that "important nonsense"—her Momma's words—would present itself and charm her away.

Toba stands and lifts the heavy bucket filled with gray water. She leads it, or more truthfully it leads her, to the front porch, where she splashes a dirty waterfall down onto the untended part of Momma's flower garden.

"Yes, this will be a day to live, a day made for a good life," Toba sighs, not envious, but noting, in much the way she has heard her Momma mouth the same words, dressed in the same apron—too big, in need of another pocket, uncomfortably starched but fragrant.

After a long moment, her hands saddled on her soft

hips, Toba releases a heavy breath, then turns from what will not be her "day made for a good life" to what has become her kitchen floor "made for a good scrubbing."

Clean now, it is nearly dry from the corner all the way to the stove. The soapy smell that will last for the rest of the morning, and somehow drift into the taste of every bite of lunch, teases her nose. With steps light and barefoot, the empty bucket swinging easy, Toba stretches her legs long and taut so that she does not have too many steps to take should she lose her balance and touch down and leave her imprint on a damp place. It is an amusing game that takes her back one step to when she was a young girl and would boast to Momma of her power to leap from the doormat and fly all the way to the stairs in one bound.

On her knees, Toba buffs the wood with a soft rag that was once a sleeve of Anna's sweater until it caught the point of a fence—or was it a razor? Toba knows Anna never much cared for the gift from Aunt Martha. The floor, like a face, loses and gains expressions under the pressure of the circling rag. Its mood changes from a cloudy dampness of doubt to a dry, certain finish and, deeper, to a smooth, smiling shine.

When she is done—or at least she hopes she is done—Toba takes what no longer can be recognized as ever having been a sweater and stands to inspect her work. She is disappointed to find that, where she had imagined the floor was even and brilliant, there are small pools and dull patches staring up at her. Around and through them are a series of dancing footprints that lead directly to where she now stands. These, of course, can only be her own—either that or they belong to a clumsy-footed ghost with just Toba's fat and crooked toes.

Toba drops two rags to the floor. She steps on each and, like skates on fine ice, glides over to the unfinished patches, where she twists and grinds her ankles as though she is putting out a small fire or killing a bug. This sliding and twisting goes on for much longer than is needed to dry those spots, but she does not stop until her knees begin to ache and she can hear the voice of her conscience, sounding much like her Momma, cough more than say, "Good enough," and then add, "Good enough for you, Toba."

Upstairs, while dusting, Toba notices the tarnished brass handle of her wardrobe is in need of polishing. This is not on the list of jobs which she was presented this morning, on a piece of paper so neatly inscribed it could have been a decree from the Czar. She considers the situation. Who cares whether this is on your list or not? You have eyes. The handle is in need of a coat—maybe two—of polish. This is what is at heart here. Toba must nod at her own ability to think a problem through. Still, she decides to ignore the thought. After all, having the talent to think out a problem to its end has opened her eyes to see that there is no one around to witness her laziness. Besides, Momma will be home soon. And should she find Toba bent over the handle, she will surely say, "So, you have decided to polish the brass as well. Very nice. So when you are finished, you will come downstairs and put that muscle to work on some other needy pieces, no?"

This is the thanks she will receive for doing more than what is called for? It is a thank-you she can do without.

The dusting goes quickly, though a thorough job it cannot be called. What is the sense? In a day, the dust, like invisible snow, will reappear as if the invention of a duster was nothing but a crazy idea even an idiot would not dare to suggest.

This is much like those foolish men who, at the first sniff of snowfall, pull on their hats and grab their brooms to sweep what is nothing more than air, for fear that even a single flake will settle on their precious dirt road. And once the cold chills them, so they are as stiff as the handles of their brooms, and the night chases them, aching, into their homes, into their warm beds, they will sleep badly, knowing they will wake to find whatever work they have done the night before useless. For the snow, like the dust, will continue to fall, never pausing to rest. These tiny nothings that even a child's breath can carry away seem to be more powerful than the strongest man, the fiercest cleaner. And the next morning, what was before a shining cabinet will be a speckled embarrassment; and the clean path, a carpet of white, crisp joy in the hands of a child and torture to the tired eyes of an adult.

And yet, knowing all that she does about snow, children and sleepless older people, Toba also knows that she must do as she has been told, which she does, moving from room to room, the chicken-feather duster flapping from her wrist over books, lanterns, jewelry boxes, candles and letters, like the tail of a crazed dog, wild and careless, spraying a fine layer of particles into the still air. She watches the specks, tiny and weightless, dance in the window's pale light.

As they perform, she finds herself—or at least her mouth—humming to their rising and circling. And when the wind from her flapping quiets, she takes delight as the dancers silently, gently, dreamily, fall until she lets the mad dog loose again, allowing the entertainers no rest. "If I am working, why should it be any different for them?"

The song Toba hums as she shakes the curtains, even after she has let the dancers bow and curtsy to the floor, strikes her ear as familiar. It is a moment before she searches and finds just where before she has heard the simple melody. She pauses, then hums it again, louder, but not rushing the tune. Yes, she is certain she has heard it before. It is her Momma's song; well, not only her Momma's. Toba has heard the song hummed—moaned, in the market, in other homes, in gardens, even on milk carts—always by workers. Often it is accompanied by the free feet of the laborers tapping the rhythm and minding the pace.

Though Toba has heard the song many times, this is the first time her ears have caught the tune coming from her own lips. She knows that this song has no words written to memorize like those in school, and yet she has heard her Momma fit words neatly to the harmony. They are usually phrases of nonsense, making light of whatever she is thinking at the moment . . . Momma might be cleaning the house, perhaps sweeping the stairway just as Toba is doing now, and Papa may call from his workroom for a glass of tea. Without stopping or straightening from her stooping, Momma will call out, sing out, in perfect measure to her humming, "Yes, Papa, your tea is boiling and you should not be surprised to find a biscuit keeping it company."

The tune, so light, free, clean, would not even hint at the strain that Momma would be placing on the yielding handle of the broom. It flows effortlessly while her body struggles, her knuckles tense and white, against a cursed stain unimpressed with her gritted teeth, glaring stare and biting bristles.

Why should such a tune exist? After all, what good reason could there be to sing about a boiling pot of tea or a biscuit, or even hum, unthinking, while your hands fight a stubborn stain for the rights to the carpet? Singing is meant to be joyful. Work is certainly no joy. The two, it seems clear, are enemies. To force them to shake hands when there is no love in their hearts for each other cannot be right. And if there is a criminal here, it is not the work, for this must get done—or so it is said (*often*, if you have a momma who considers dirt a cruel, unwelcome intruder). No, the enemy here is the song; this liar, this mocker, making a fool of the body's struggles by telling the world that the acts of scrubbing, sweeping, polishing, are ones not of drudgery, of torture, but of pride, choice, even passion!

If the mouth must make a noise at such a time, Toba would understand a groan, a series of endless "tsk-tsks," a plea for help—but a song? It is wrong, wrong.

Toba has proof to back such strong and vital thinking. Proof like the first book of the Torah. It was commanded that man shall earn bread "by the sweat of his brow." This was his punishment for eating from the tree of knowledge, the fruit that was forbidden to be tasted. Such punishment cannot be ignored, not when it comes from this source. And to try and lighten His words, to make the load that much more bearable, to pretend that there is no pain in work, is to insult Him. This, of course, is a sin.

These are the thoughts that have run deep in Toba for long years, and continue to run as she rubs the corner of an oil-soaked rag into a deep scratch in the banister. And yet, as the wound seems to heal itself under her touch, she is also continuing her song, "Yes, darling, better, better yet."

Has she changed her mind? Has the river that has steadily run through her, singing the song against work, changed course? Who can tell? She is working, not thinking. And when she walks down the stairway which she has swept until the grain in the wood looks like the coat of a well-brushed colt, she pauses at each step, one, then another, feeling much the way a bride must feel walking down the aisle. She does not care to find a word to express what she is feeling—though if she were forced, it would have to be "pride." She knows, of course, that she has not created a great work of art, nor has she saved a threatened life. A clean floor is little more than what it is—a clean floor. All she has done is wash where there was dirt, smooth what was rough and shine the dull. But, still, *not* to admit her feeling, *not* to hum it, *not* to sing it, would be a greater lie than to deny it. "You are a fine, deep wood."

So what does this mean? Could it mean that all of a sudden—in the time that the birds have taken to wake and sing in full voice their morning chorus—Toba has learned to appreciate what her Momma has always said she would never learn? No, this cannot be true or she would not now be passing by a stray spoon trapped under the foot of the stove. Is it that she likes everything orderly, everything in its place, tidy and neat? One look at the blouse half in and half out of her skirt answers that question. Does it mean anything more than a song—for no other reason than it had the notion—found its way into her ear and there settled only to be freed by her tongue? And if this is true, then could this song from the lips have little if anything to do with the lifting of her load, the easing of the tired, sore joints of her overworked body?

Whatever it means, Toba continues to work on the piece before her with gentle strokes, breathing years back into her Papa's aged chest of drawers. "Do you remember how strong you were? How fierce?" To a silver-etched candlestick she croons, "You must be steamed, not to harm your precious skin." And to her Papa, returning home from shul, she calls out, loud and chiming, "Good morning, Papa. Momma will be home soon—that is, if she has not been made a prisoner by the Janken sisters' tongues."

Toba is mystified at how her hands keep so busy and perfectly aimed while her voice frees her spirit. But, still, the true test remains. It will come when Momma returns and calls out from the kitchen her review of Toba's floor. And should she call out that it is "good enough," Toba will sing back, in the tune of the song of work, "Good enough for Toba."

The Stranger

I

Toba wills herself deaf. It is a simple trick, one she finds that, as she grows older, she must perform more and more often. By busying her hands—now smoothing a wrinkle that does not exist in her dress—and capturing the attention of her eyes to focus on the painfully slow hand movements of the wall clock, Toba's ears harden into stone. They hear everything, but listen to not a word.

". . . And so here, miss, here is where it is most important to give special care," Mrs. Kerchival continues, her voice pinching higher to announce concern, her eyes narrowing to demonstrate precision, her aged fingers stretching and pricking with strained patience to show once again the way it is done. "With practice, it is not so impossible, no?"

"No," Toba responds.

Teacher and student are somewhere along their third lesson, though neither could say with any certainty just where the student stands on the road to mastery.

"See how simple?"

Toba does not look.

The instrument causing Toba such torture—and Mrs. Kerchival equal misery, seeing her pupil attack when she is told to coax—is not a piano or harp or a musical instrument at all. Though to Toba, this is no hardship, since she has learned from Moshe Dermin, the boy with the birthmark which seems to nibble his lower lip, that there is no joy in studying music, either. "After so many times striking the same keys," Moshe told her, turning his head and lowering his voice, for his momma was nearby and known to have the ears of a wolf and a temper as dangerous, "even music becomes noise." No, this is not a piano which sits before Toba, or, more properly ordered, as Mrs. Kerchival would only have it, which Toba sits before. It is a sewing machine. Coal-black, shining, perfect.

"This, miss, you will attempt."

Toba's fingers, usually capable of performing most any task, stiffen like stale noodles before the loud, wheezing beast whom Mrs. Kerchival talks to, strokes with her handkerchief, adores as if it were her loving, possibly slow-witted, child.

"How it dances! Up-down! Up-down!" the teacher sings, her fingers twitching, delighted. "More quickly it sews than a man. More gracefully, too. And you will never prick your finger again. *Poof*!" She breathes out a gust of meaty air.

Toba does not *ohh* and *ahh*. She does not shudder with temptation, as she is told others do. Nor does she wonder at the great treasures which she hears this new machine will, like a thief, reach out for and carry back to her. She does not believe that she is a "very fortunate young woman . . ." (she knows Mrs. Kerchival says "young woman," but thinks "small child") ". . . to have parents who pay money to have their daughter learn such a fine art." And above all, she does not want to "execute fancy stitches that knot the fingers of even the most skilled tailors."

What does she want? Well, if she were asked, Toba would not hesitate to answer. And words would not be necessary to communicate her deep feelings. A simple kick would do—sending the whole contraption, table and all, to the floor, where its "miraculous" parts could crack, break, spring loose, with the mightiest of crashes.

"*That*," she would tell Moshe Dermin and his feared momma, "is *true* music!"

"No! No, miss, you must let the machine work. You

are too . . . too firm. Too wooden—like a tree, yes? Do not worry so. The machine—it is smarter than you, smarter than me, yes?" The question, posed at least twice each lesson, always followed by the once amusing, then tiresome, now sickening laugh, is this time punctuated by the teacher grasping and leading the student's hand to the body of the trembling machine. Toba's fingers, like frightened worms, crawl inward for protection, forming a fist.

The laughter stops. The machine growls.

Mrs. Kerchival quickly frees her grip and awkwardly, in the manner of one picking himself up from a fall before a crowd, stumbles for words. "Yes . . . I-I . . . Did you know that, miss, everyone in the great city of Dansk sews in this fashion? Yes, yes. This shawl, it was made at the hands of this very machine. Lovely thing . . . lovely."

To this sad song, Toba's ears soften, as do her fingers, which reach out and stroke the shawl. She speaks in the broken words of her teacher. "Lovely . . . lov-e-ly."

The lesson continues until, as in the previous sessions, Toba, with affected innocence high in her voice, calls to Mrs. Kerchival's attention that somehow their two hours have passed. But the long-awaited breath of relief quickly sours. For, though the act which she must now perform is in many ways more simple than any asked of her all morning, Toba finds what she is about to do almost too painful.

Head bowed, unable to bear the savage stare of the

machine—no doubt relishing her anguish—Toba reaches into her purse to find the knotted handkerchief sewn by her Papa, heavy with coins. Cautiously, in the manner she had this morning received the coins at the hands of her Momma, Toba counts each ruble—not silently but aloud, not twice but three times.

Knowing that she must appear to be pitifully stingy, Toba continues to hold, to weigh, her teacher's payment as her mind hungrily searches for just the method of making four coins appear as five. When the laws of mathematics and physics prove unyielding, she finally places each coin, one by one, onto the well-oiled table, with a click aimed to scratch.

II

Of course there were rumors. But all strangers—even old widows, if indeed they truly are widows—bring these along with every trunk they have carried, every piece of clothing they wear, each button missing from their collars (this also holds true for pieces of furniture, aged books and, especially, framed photographs of people who did not accompany the strangers on their journeys).

And, of course, it is the work, duty, pleasure—all—of the townspeople to add their personal thoughts, fears, facts, suspicions, to every article seen, heard of, predicted. This, Toba considers more than simple gossip, but a ritual, passed down from very old directly to very young—mysteriously missing those in the middle, too busy for what Toba's Papa claims to be "idle minds straining to create waste."

One such rumor concerning the Stranger from Dansk was that she had been the lover of the czar but had fallen from his grace once her beauty had faded. Another favorite was that the stranger did not leave Dansk on her own, but was chased out by the authorities because her husband—whom they caught and imprisoned, possibly starved—was a traitor. Then there were the stories of how the stranger had not come from Dansk at all, but from some place far away—so far that this place had no name. The stranger had fled from that place and had come to Lenchintz for the purpose of forgetting. And what she was said to be forgetting was an ever-widening river of Lenchintz's separate and combined miseries, illnesses, failures, lost dreams and curses.

Toba herself, on several occasions, had come running home, her breath panting far behind, to announce the truth about Mrs. Kerchival, the Stranger from Dansk. On one such occasion she had learned from not one but a crowd of sources—some, she knew, were not at all trustworthy—that the old widow was not a widow at all.

"She is not even *old*!" Toba said, with great certainty.

"That's right, Toba," Papa had said. "She is not old, and I am not listening."

But talk Toba did of how the stranger was in truth a smooth-skinned maiden who, out of hatred for her life, had become wrinkled and bitter.

"Ach!" Toba's Papa had growled, his face turned pale, as if he'd swallowed something foul. "Just to ruin each other. This is why we are born."

"But, Papa," Momma had said, coming to her daughter's as well as her own defense, for she, too, had a theory as to Mrs. Kerchival's true past, "is it not true when a child is brought into this world he is first checked for sickness? So why should this not be so for a stranger in a new land?"

Papa had nodded this way and that, with each bend in his wife's logic, not sure, not unsure, only certain that he had no taste for what he called a woman's sour tongue.

There was, however, one real mystery which did follow the Stranger from Dansk—one that kept even Papa wondering, though silently. Like all true mysteries, the stranger's offered a clue. A wooden chest, artfully carved and embellished with brass latches and handles, with gilded edges fashioned into leaves, nuts, fruits and small animals. The chest—which the stranger had watched over as if it held all the world's hopes while two large men mumbled and carried it from the carriage into the house—was the like of which Lenchintz had never before seen.

"Never mind Lenchintz," said Mrs. Lubeshnitz, a collector of everything. "In all of Poland such a box can't be found."

"What could be so precious that the woman nearly prays to it?" asked a mother, picking up her heavy son to see.

"Jewels," someone offered from the growing crowd.

"In such a large chest that causes even the muscles of those men to tremble? Rocks, I could believe. Stones, perhaps. Jewels—never."

"Perfumes, then?" a man's voice questioned, more than told.

"No," said Moshe Dermin's momma, and everyone nodded, for she not only possessed the ears of a wolf but the nose of one as well.

"What then?" they asked, turning to one another, baffled.

A full week had passed before Lenchintz was made a present of the knowledge concerning the contents of the chest belonging to the Stranger from Dansk. And all that wondering, worrying, questioning, guessing, was settled with one simple question, asked by one simple fisherman.

"What kind of fish is that one, Mr. Helber?" Mrs. Kerchival had asked, pointing to a blue-eyed, silver-flecked carp.

"This I will tell you," answered the fisherman, known for few words, "if you tell me what it is that you keep inside your crate."

And so it was told, heard and quickly retold again and again until finally the basket weaver asked, "A sewing machine? What is this *sewing machine*?"

"Tickets you could sell!" said Mrs. Letchen, fanning herself with her hand, somewhere outside the house of the stranger. She, like everyone else in Lenchintz and towns quite a distance away, had stopped what they were doing to come, stand, listen, talk, move and chat some more, as they inched closer along the line that would lead them to this wonder of wonders.

Once inside the crowded house, elbows cutting like saws for extra room, the Stranger from Dansk performed. Obviously embarrassed and uncomfortable, she stitched, or rather watched the machine stitch, in mere moments what would have taken a great tailor his best effort to create. At such a sight many closed their eyes and began to pray, others trembled as if freezing—the sweat rising from their necks—and the weak-blooded naturally fainted to the floor.

"A curse," they said.

"A demon!" they pointed.

"A creature from the other world." They stepped back.

This continued until the very old rabbi, who rarely left his shul, was brought to look, ponder and settle this unholy matter that had for some unthinkable reason found its way into peaceful, sleeping Lenchintz. Those who were close enough witnessed a most bizarre sight. Here was the great rabbi, a scholar, a healer, a teacher, gray and unsteady, beside this shining, smooth, foreign object, solid and unimpressed.

After great study, with long moments of pause to turn and confer with his large, worn, leather-bound books, the rabbi faced the still crowd and revealed to them the pure truth about what was now, at the end of the line, called "the Curse of Kerchival."

In his small, shaking voice, he told them, "What we have here, my good friends, I must tell you, is a sewing machine."

Not knowing what to do—except for the fainters, who, what else?, collapsed—the people bowed their heads and hushed, "Amen."

And so it went as it always goes. This "catastrophe," this "sign from beyond," this "warning," this "plague," was soon accepted, quickly befriended and immediately forgotten. Perhaps this occured more quickly than it would have, since, in the following month, Mrs. Geldeman's daughter Julie had given birth to twins—both boys—and Mr. Sabine's accident caused him to speak in a language that no one understood. It was just as the rabbi had said, a sewing machine. And she was just as she said, a stranger from Dansk.

And now Lenchintz had a new neighbor to chat with as they hung laundry on the line, another old lady who paid boys with sweets to carry her groceries, an advisor to the newly married women, a friend to all, a teacher to one.

All this Toba struggles to understand, along with a feeling that frightens her, as she makes her short journey back to her house longer with legs that seem weighted down as if rooted.

III

"So, my prize-winning seamstress, what is it that you taught this machine today?" Toba's Papa calls out from his workshop as soon as the front door opens. Quickly he follows with words which, though light with laughter, cut deep to Toba's heart. "But, then, what more can a machine learn when they say it already makes a man's hands useless?"

Toba does not answer either question. She stands outside the unlit room, hearing her Papa's laughter quiet to restful breaths. It is as if there is a wall, a door or a wind pushing her back, not allowing her to enter his room, forbidding Toba to get close to her Papa. How can she tell him about this machine? Perhaps, she thinks, this is the reason why God has taken his sight—so he will not have to witness the cruel beauty this sewing machine creates.

"It is a stupid beast—this machine!" Toba forces out, and finds herself nearly running into the room. "It is uglier than the Permins' cow and more stupid than the Fedlers' mule!"

"Last time," her Papa laughs, holding out his hands in the direction of Toba's voice, "it was the Permins' stupid cow and the Felders' ugly mule."

Toba does not laugh at her Papa's joke. It only adds wood to her anger's fire.

"Your sewing is *much* finer. Even with the dullest needles and coarsest threads!" Toba shouts, grabbing her

Papa's hands and rubbing them as if they are frozen, wishing into them the power, the dance, she knows beats in the metal heart of the Stranger from Dansk's machine.

"Ahh, my adoring Tobala," her Papa sighs. "My Tobala. You should not be so harsh—even on 'a stupid beast.' " He nods. She does not. "Soon enough, before your glowing eyes, it will grow from ugly to beautiful, from stupid to a scholar. The whole world will change soon. You will see. When you look from America."

Toba's hands stop their rubbing. They fall lifeless onto her Papa's lap. More than ever, more than the months before Bella left, even more than those months that followed slowly after she'd gone, it seems every word, every thought, everything, means *America*. And lately it has gotten so that in their home in Lenchintz, in Poland, the Cohens—all but Toba—have *become* Americans. It seems that they are trying, straining, to pull this great, foreign land, this new world, closer, as if they have in their hands a cord and on the other end is America, a great ship, being drawn toward them to dock and carry Toba off.

This is even true of Toba's Momma who, after she read one letter from Bella about the meals in America, began to serve the Cohens what she called, in a voice full of childish laughter, American style. Bella had written that in America they eat a heavy meal late and a lighter, cold meal midday. The following afternoon, Toba looked down at her plate and saw dinner, or what would ordinarily be dinner. And when she looked at her Papa, certain he would straighten out this foolishness, all she saw was her Papa eating his meal, contentedly, unconcerned whether it was dinner, lunch, late or early.

And the problem did not end just there. With each letter, another change would arrive, pulling the great ship ever closer. Tea, not in a glass, but in a cup "is the way it is taken in America" and now it was so in the Cohens' home. And to go along with the glass, the sugar was stirred into the cup, no longer held between the teeth and drunk through as they did it all over the world except in this crazy New World. And with each change, with each pull, with each argument from Toba, all was settled with the word, "America." *America*.

Now, with the coming of the stranger's machine of miracles, the problem became unbearable. The machine, the lessons, the payments, the acceptance of strange ways, was overwhelming. Like a terrible wave it rose high and strong, roared like a beast, drowning Toba. But worse than that, this wave carried on its back to Lenchintz the great ship America. Shining, ghostly, impossible to deny.

"This sewing machine," says her Papa, taking hold of Toba's hands, "it is a dream machine. More than clothing, it weaves a tapestry of dreams. And like a dream, Toba, it will carry you off to a beautiful place. A beautiful life."

Feeling the hope strong in his hands, seeing the calm of peace in his face, smelling that scent which has always meant safe, love, forever, Toba kneels and rests her head on his lap and hushes, "Yes, Papa."

IV

By the time the rumor reaches Toba, it has already grown from an unsteady whisper to a choked question, from shocked faces to pointed fingers, from disbelieving hisses to one hardened fact.

In the market, her basket heavy with green vegetables, salt, potatoes and a chicken, all to be boiled for that night's "lunch," Toba overhears Mrs. Serentiski moaning about "the tragedy of the Stranger from Dansk." Toba's eyes turn from one of the baker's famed raisin cakes to the cross-eyed woman, who speaks with both pride and pity in her voice.

"The poor woman . . . poor, poor woman . . ." she breathes out, loud enough for those across the market to hear. "A sin . . . a terrible, terrible thing . . ."

Finally, seeing that she has a respectable audience, living proof that *she*, Ida Serentiski, the woman who has never received her due for being the first to tell of the Rimmers' five-legged calf, is indeed the first to bring forth this "tsk, tsk, horrible, awful" news.

"Listen," she begins. "I wasn't there, of course. How could I be? If I were there, such a thing would never have happened, true? Of course, true. But what happened I know like it happened to me—like it happened to my grandchild—this I can tell you. What happened? Mrs. Kerchival arrived, the poor dear, from buying her daily loaf—a pumpernickel it was, I believe—and what did she find? . . ." Mrs. Serentiski pauses, adding to the tension, and the crowd—like professional actors—takes its cue beautifully.

"To find her house had burned to cinders!" one guesses.

Mrs. Serentiski does not answer, only dabs her fat tears and shakes her head.

"To find her cat had died, the poor thing," another offers.

"She has no cat!" someone corrects.

Mrs. Serentiski merely whimpers and sighs.

"To find her husband had come for her!" calls the baker.

"Yes! Sure! Of course!" the crowd calls out, congratulating the baker.

"No!" Mrs. Serentiski shouts. "It was her machine!"

"Stolen!" the entire marketplace calls out, then falls as silent as the moment following thunder. And it is here that short, plump Ida Serentiski rises high on her thick legs, catching in one glance all their eyes so as to carve a picture in their minds. "The machine was not stolen, it was . . . *crippled*!"

The crowd, as if one solid mass, steps back. Ida Serentiski is pleased.

"Crippled? Did I say crippled?" she asks, sure that no one could possibly answer. "I mean *destroyed*! The parts, this woman found, were broken all over her house. Her table, too! And that lovely chest—now a memory. This was no accident. I can tell you. The poor, poor, poor woman."

The words, now spoken strong and full, cast a spell over the market. Even the wind, mischievously teasing kerchiefs and dresses, now behaves. Not one mouth speaks. Not one body moves. Not even the weak-blooded fainters. Except for Toba, who, though still tempted by the baker's raisin cakes, turns to carry that night's meal back to her home, hearing the words of her Momma's warning, "Be quick as a thief in the night."

V

If there are any further rumors, they go unspoken, unheard, and are most probably unthinkable. No one even dares to guess. The police haven't a single clue. Neighbors have seen nothing. Lenchintz offers no answers, only words of comfort, "shame, pity, sin, punishment."

"My poor darling," Momma says for days after the tragedy. "This loss is yours more than anyone else's."

Toba never nods, nor does she disagree, but only understands, or tries to understand, what had before made clear and perfect sense. It is as if she herself is a stranger who has only heard of, or possibly witnessed, the crime. She can close her eyes and see the house. The inside empty. And the machine. Its back to her, still. Not buzzing, not pounding. An infant sleeping, unaware and innocent.

By the time the people of the market have rushed over to pay the mourner their respect, Mrs. Kerchival has disappeared. She has left everything behind but the parts of the machine. The fact that no one saw her leave, unlocked the greatest flood of rumors Lenchintz has ever heard. Rumors that make the Stranger from Dansk more spirit than flesh, more shadow that living.

"She ran in the direction of Kiev, her hair flaming!"

"She is still in the woods, working in a blistering fever to put the machine back together with the help of the demons that live in rocks and trees."

"She did not run. She vanished in an instant. From the shock, she went up in smoke."

Silently, Toba listens as the storm of such rumors rises. And in her silence she wrestles with her own stranger, one who, like a dream, is gone before it can be remembered, and yet remains always. To Toba, this stranger is much like the place, the ship—America—now pushed back where it belongs, across an ocean said to be both a giver and a taker of life.

The Horse

The horse and the girl share the lantern's oily glow. Swaying to the steady back and forth of the carriage, the yellow light offers just enough of the future for the mare to move ahead, and so much of the past that Toba's mind may retreat to again visit the scene at the train station where she, her Papa and her Momma parted.

"What is to worry? So you know—I put in your bag a warm sweater. As for the laundry, it will be here waiting for you to come home. This is a promise!" Toba smiles broadly, sadly.

"Three days—four," Momma promises, asks, apologizes.

The train shivers, belches clouds of steam and coughs impatiently.

"Yetta, go now." Papa reaches for her hand.

Momma gives her left hand while her right nervously braids Toba's thick hair.

"It will be fine," Toba orders. "Tell Anna I want a nephew this time—with *my* eyes. And you tell her husband. . ."

The train's whistle blows, sending the birds flapping into the air, and Toba's words following. There is a final squeeze, a look. Then, hurrying, Momma turns to lift her patched bag. The conductor takes her by the arm and helps her up onto the metal steps, into the black belly of the train.

The news had arrived in a letter. Anna's second child is to come at the pain of a hard birth; so the doctor says. What could Momma do? Toba asks herself, now braiding the leather reins in her hands. Nothing. Still, she agrees with the horse's ever-bobbing head, it is good that Momma goes.

Toba turns to her Papa. He is quiet, more than usual. It comes to her that silence has different sounds. There is the lazy, musical quiet of rest, heard on the Sabbath. There is the sharp sound before something is about to happen, good or bad, like when you sit in the dentist's chair or smell something that must taste wonderful. But worst of all is the silence of unknowing. This is her Papa's silence as they ride through the night in the carriage rented from Mr. Kelmer for "a very good price."

"Everything will be fine." "There will be rain tomorrow." "I can smell the fat clouds." "Momma will be home before we will, if this horse does not decide to use its legs."

These are just some words of nonsense Toba could use to lift the terrible weight of the silence of unknowing. But she keeps her lips tight as her hands are on the sweating leather straps she uses to steer the tired horse. Such forced words would only call attention to the awful stillness, and make things worse. It is the same with the finger's inability to leave alone a hardening scab, or the tongue's torture of a bad tooth.

And so they continue, barely moving, not speaking, hardly even thinking, until somewhere along the dull road, the horse raises its head and whinnies. The reins are nearly pulled from Toba's hands, and she from her seat. She stands and leans backward, pulling with all her strength, stopping the carriage with a jolt. The lantern swings hard, throwing the weak light about the dark woods lining the road.

This could be the perfect break in the silence—what better topic of conversation than a crazy horse acting up in the middle of the night in the middle of God-knows-where? But the fact remains that the silence remains. Toba feels it grow heavier.

She struggles to keep calm, but lets her anger out, bringing the whip down hard on the horse's neck. The strap smacks with a stinging sound, yet brings no movement. Toba tries again. Nothing but an echo. Now she gives a bit of a holler, low and deep, trying to sound like the voice of Mr. Kelmer. But the problem is the horse responds just as she has seen her respond to Mr. Kelmer—with a bored cough.

Toba turns to her Papa, who seems to be nodding—to what she does not know. She knows he cannot possibly think they have arrived home—so why such a gesture? She turns to the horse, who at this moment might be the most sensible of the three, and gives her another good crack with the reins. The sound only returns to smack Toba's ear.

Now what? Again she looks at her Papa. Yes, he is nodding. The only conclusion she can possibly draw is that the horse, who refuses to move, and her Papa, who refuses to speak, have an understanding. A deal. Maybe there has not been silence this whole trip, but a great dialogue between the horse and man. A deep discussion she cannot hear. But she knows what her Papa would say to this. "Is it that you cannot hear or that you were not listening?"

Toba bites down on her lip and lets loose a strong hit with the straps. The horse is stone.

"Come now! We are late as it is," Toba talks at her, forcing a kind tone. "The journey is not over. We are not yet home." But the horse is playing the part of a mule. How can she possibly make this stupid beast understand that she is hungry, that her back aches from their dull, thudding pace and that her Papa is so worried about his daughter he cannot speak? Then, for what reason she doubts she will ever know, Toba realizes she does not know the animal's name. She thinks. But it is fruitless. She has never once heard Mr. Kelmer call the mare anything but curses—no, this is not true, either. She has heard him be very kind to her as well. But how could he not name her—the one he has ridden for countless years, the one who is forced to listen to his braggings, his miseries, the one by whose labor he feeds his family? Toba thinks about Anna's baby. By now it could be that he is already born. They do not name the child until days after the birth—for reasons of luck, she supposes. But to leave a creature nameless is a terrible crime. Enough! Name or no name, this horse must again begin its slow pounding.

Kind words. Mean words. Songs. Jokes. Beatings. Names like "chicken," "numskull," "lazy." Feeding him an apple, which he eats greedily . . . Toba tries everything. She is about to cry, to scream, when there is a laugh. Loud and deep. It is the first human sound, other than her own, Toba has heard since this afternoon's crowded train station.

"When I was a young man—it was so long ago that I must have been young—I had a horse. Her name, as I remember, was Sadie Greenfield, but this was also the name of my friend Herschel's mother so I could be mistaken. It seems to me now they both had chestnut eyes—but this is another story, yes? Well, it happens this day I must make an errand for my papa. A load of wood from the next town. I remember the cold being a terrible thing. Like the claw of an animal, it ripped off your hat, and through your coat into a poor boy's flesh. Call me a liar, it is the way it was. Well, of course, Sadie decided along this winter road we should stop. We should rest a while as the snow fell and covered us like a grave. 'Why not? If we are to freeze, this is certainly a fine place for it.' This is what I said to Sadie. But such wit was wasted on the poor girl, who could dance nicely, but never had an ear for lively conversation. So there she stood, still, like she was having a photograph taken, the snow filling her ears, falling over her eyes and, of course, not missing me at all. I coaxed her, pulled her ears, offered to carry her on my back, promised her a cooked breakfast each morning—nothing. It did no good. She would come when she would go. And that was that. We had to wait nearly two hours in such a storm for Sadie to be cold enough that she would decide to move on. Two hours! Two days! Years! I was sure I would never be seen again. And when I was found—it would be Lazar Cohen, the frozen boy with a beard of snow and a nose of ice! Sadie—my Sadie!"

He laughs loud. Tears, fat and sparkling, rest in his beard. The horse joins in the laughter, throwing her head around, jingling her chains in applause. Toba is stunned. Only on holidays—when company is around—does her

Papa ever speak in such tones, for such lengths of time. It is even rarer when he speaks of himself. This story is a first for Toba's ears.

And of all places to reveal such a tale—such a truth—in the middle or end—God forbid not just the beginning!—of a dark road, trying to get this stubborn, nameless mare to move.

Imagine the look on a stranger's face—if he could see in the dark—witnessing such a sight. A mare that won't pull. A girl strapping the horse's back. And an old man filling the world with his life's stories.

The thought sparks Toba's anger. *She* will not wait for the horse to decide when and if they go—even if this was her Papa's way. *She* is the master. And the horse is the worker. She takes firm hold of the reins now and without even a wince, lets them come down hard again and again on the horse's back, neck, cheek. When the sounds die in the air, Toba finds herself just where she was, only more upset. The only change is in her Papa, who is no longer nodding. Good, she thinks, he has come to his senses. Then, right before her eyes, he begins shaking his head from side to side, as if to say, "poor, pitiful horse." Or worse, "poor, pitiful Toba."

Again she cracks the whip. Again the horse stands her ground, reaching out her long neck, as she eats the weeds that grow thick and high from the road's side, taunting Toba with a larger target to beat.

"When it is all said, we must eat. To tell us to do

otherwise is a waste of strength and words. The mind cannot hear when the stomach whispers." The voice is gentle, distant yet carries a stern hand forcing back the next blow from falling. "These blind eyes have seen men with families dead, their houses cinders, still smoking, beg not to cover their wounds, not to clothe their nakedness, but for food. This is the greatest healer of all. It gives our body rest. It offers our minds the medicine of sleep, our souls some hope, some small joy. Smaller, it is true, when the food is cold and tasteless, no?" He smiles, amused. Toba, too, smiles, the braids in her hands now still and lax. How strange. Her Papa, his voice seemingly freed by the horse's fit of stubbornness, the night air and the loneliness. Now the weight of the silence is lifted high. His voice pushes and reaches like powerful hands. It is as if the horse has known him all her life and has taken this moment to say, "Talk, old friend. I will listen."

His stories follow each other, jumping each other, blending, like a stream overflowing with color and freshness. They swim over Toba, clean and fast.

Stories of the day he learned what the covenant of the circumcision was. "There I was, holding my older brother Alex's son. What was I—a baby myself." And when the mohel uncovered the blade, poor Lazar had to "pray as hard as I ever did to keep steady and not faint before the rabbi and the entire congregation. For weeks I ached at just the thought."

Then there was the first meal Momma had ever cooked—or, as he said, "burned" for him. "I had come home from work. In those days I had just a little shop—*Lazar Cohen, Tailor*—and there she was, my wife. Something to get used to. After all, I had never been married before and she was so pretty—and me, I was the perfect fool. So there we were, man and wife. She made me wash my hands, then had me change out of my work shirt into a robe—this is how she treated me. And then she presented me with the meat—brisket, I think it was. Well, whatever it was, I remember the color—dark as firewood after it is burnt. And she was so proud. Of course I ate it all, and complained on and on until she laughed when there was not any more left."

There was the story of Anna's sickness that lasted three weeks. A fever that ate at her until she weighed forty pounds. The time Momma invited her whole family for Purim, "and, wouldn't you know, they all came!" Then there was the story of the night before Toba was born—when a dream had come to him. "I have had many dreams before and after this night, but none to match the face—a vision, it was—that visited me that night. The face of an angel. The face of my Toba. And the words you spoke—a prophet. 'Dark jewel.' These are the words you spoke. And here you are. My jewel. And here I am, blind. Yes, yes, you are my dark jewel."

On and on, a loving and feeling river. Toba listens and the horse listens and the woods listen to the tales of a blind man, whose voice is rarely heard, now confess his sins, complain of his misfortune, laugh at his gifts, his faults, and hold firm to his dreams.

Toba listens with the ear of a wife, of a mother, a friend, a stranger. A daughter.

Through it all the horse eats, belches, kicks, bobs her head and stares on, the yellow light dim and comfortable. And though they are not moving, Toba feels as if she is on a journey, turning with the road of each tale. Sometimes she is pushed ahead, then she is floating backward, taken with the current of her Papa's tone, never knowing what is coming next. The burial of his momma. The year he studied with the great rabbi of Vilna. The pogroms.

He is a peddler, taking from his worn bag the pieces of his life. He breathes on each, rubbing to give even a rusted year a shine. One by one, each story—another ware—he displays for the world to see, to consider, to weigh, in this utter darkness.

Toba remains still; the straps, worn smooth from her futile struggling, hang loose and free about the horse's ears. What else can she possibly do? With a mare who refuses to believe there is another inch of road to travel, and a Papa who is content to sit and talk, she has little choice.

Then, slowly, in the way a storm begins and ends with light, sweet drops, the stories fall into a silence, the words remain light as a mist in the air; what is left is not the silence of laziness, though clearly music can be heard. It is not the sharp silence of moments before something is about to happen, though there is a feeling Toba recognizes as a beginning. And it is not the terrible weight of the silence of the unknowing. How could it be? She has just sat through countless lessons, and now knows her Papa in a way she could never have imagined. Yet, she would be a liar if she were to say that she has any idea of what is going to happen next.

So it is. Tonight, just where she cannot say, a new silence is born. Scented, airy, wise and peaceful. More than she hears it, Toba sees this silence. It is a bridge, built sturdy, with roots deep. On it, this night, her Papa has traveled long and alone to find himself in the dark, beside his daughter, on a strange road.

There are words in Toba's mouth, meaningless words. "You have lived a wondrous life." "Papa, I did not know such things." "I hope that somehow Momma, Anna and the baby could hear your stories." But these words are swallowed. They would only spoil this newborn silence. It is clear to Toba, as it has been long understood by the horse, that at such a time words are useless.

So now there is nothing to be done. The moon has seen all it cares to for one night and is about to close its silver eye. The woods are filled with a voice whose stories will echo in this new silence forever. The man is still and quiet. The girl holds the reins. They wait for the horse to decide to take them home.

The Fool

"Toba is happy. Toba the Beautiful is happy."

Vishna's eyes roll loosely in his head, hurrying to greet everyone and everything about him. He bows to Papa, smiles at the glass of pickles, winks at the table salt.

"I like Toba's nose. This is very tasty food, Mrs. Cohen, isn't it? Better than Mrs. Helber's brisket, which I must tell you is the best she can make." Vishna talks with his mouth full. His hands fly about, fingers twisting, reaching, touching this and that, steadying what is still, frightening the dishes so they tremble.

The other eaters pay little attention. Only Toba notices, studies his every crooked movement. It is useless, she knows from years of such study, to find a pattern.

Of all the words Vishna does not know, one for sure is *habit*. There are times he might have the eye believe his hands were blessed with the skill of a musician's or a surgeon's—they are capable of that much expression and precision—but less than a moment later those hands will lose their cunning, their speed, and like pieces of clay under the sun, they melt, shapeless.

Toba follows the tangled weave of Vishna's whiskers, red and wiry, springing up like misguided roots from the rough soil of his face. She watches him struggle with his meat, hears him ask himself whether to chew or to swallow, whether to slice the bread or bite through the crust of the entire loaf, what the proper words are following a belch loud enough to make the fork in Momma's hand shake. And she notices something else. How small he is. Could he be shrinking? There was a time, so recent she does not have to call on her memory, when she would measure herself against him. Now, even if he stood on a chair, Toba would have to look down on Vishna.

"Another piece of chicken?" Momma asks, taking up his plate before he can say "yes" or "maybe" or "could I say no to such an offer?" She places on it a leg and two slices of white breast. "Potatoes?" She lifts the ladle from the steaming pot and rolls two heavy ones to the side of the meat. "Gravy, of course." She pours the thick brown sauce over the meal and, pleased with her performance and the aromas, places the second helping before him, careful not to set the plate too near the table's edge.

"Ahhh. Thank you. Too good. A blessing. Such flavor, wasted on this tongue, tsk, tsk. Thank you."

"It is you who deserve thanks, Vishna," Papa says, reaching his hand to the guest's shoulder. "You give us a mitzvah with your company. And your carvings are a treasure to us. This one, I believe, is your finest yet."

There is a pause.

"Why—why—thank you, Reb Cohen," Vishna hushes, bowing his head. It is a sign of respect that touches Toba deeply. "Toba looks so pretty tonight. Maybe, it could be, I don't know, the spring. Yes, a flower she is. So sweet, Reb Cohen. A liar you cannot call me."

Papa nods and smiles.

It is Thursday at the Cohens' home. The three eaters take their dinner, surrounding a human storm: rocking, talking, drinking, spilling, laughing. Toba imagines the same scene with Vishna every night as he travels through Lenchintz, from table to table, house to house, to take his meals.

"Toba is big now. Bigger she is than Vishna. Soon she will be married. Soon. A day to be cherished." Vishna talks on, filling his mouth, his beard and his shirt with Momma's food. "She will marry Vishna."

Papa raises his head.

"We will live quiet lives, simple lives. Toba the Beautiful and ugly old Vishna."

"Vishna," Papa warns.

He does not hear.

"And if God's will will be done, we will be blessed with children. Let them have their mother's eyes, her nose, brains—please, God, bless them with nothing from their papa but his good fortune."

"Enough!" Papa shouts.

Vishna does not stop his words or his chewing. It is as if he is speaking from a dream.

"What will be their names? Such a question I cannot answer. A matter for their momma. A wise woman. A glowing spirit."

"Vishna!" Papa roars, releasing the knife in his hand. "You must go now."

Toba stands.

Without question, without even stopping his loud chewing, Vishna reaches over to the wall, where the cane he has carved leans. He takes it into his bony hands, shifts all his weight onto his side and lands softly on the floor. His first steps are small, frightened, as if he is testing the coat of a freshly frozen pond. But once certain that it is indeed wood beneath him and that it will not give way under him, he turns to the table and bows deeply.

"I thank you, Reb Cohen. And thank you, Mrs. Cohen. Thank you, Toba, for letting me into your holy home. For feeding me with such food and kindness I do not deserve. A blessing on your house and the house of your children." And with a hop he has turned around, and is out the front door, a faint, unfamiliar song floating from his lips.

The sound of the closing door is sharp. It echoes to Toba her Papa's rudeness. She waits for his excuse. He offers none. She looks to her Momma to right this wrong. She only presses Toba's arm.

Toba burns to speak. Her words bite at her timid tongue. But she cannot free them. Though she despises her weakness, all she can do is lift her Momma's hand from her arm and run to the door, calling loudly the name of their dismissed guest.

She finds Vishna only a few steps from the porch. It is no surprise. Toba knows the difficulty he has walking. How much pain even his tiny strides cause. But what she is surprised by is his laughing face. The wrinkles, like smoke in the wind, rise and fall with such ease. And his legs, dancing a broken step—the right an enemy of the left, knocking and tripping it up.

"Blessed is Vishna!" he sings to the moon. "Blessed be the world as Vishna is blessed!"

Vishna the fool. Vishna the pity. Vishna the pauper. The hermit. Man-child. Living joke. Sad reminder. Vishna the fool of Lenchintz waves his cane, giggles, burps, cries, stumbles before the eyes of Toba and the world.

Why should I be amazed? Toba asks herself. Is he not always carrying on so? Even in a rainstorm, Vishna is not only bound to feel the sun's heat but has been known to pull his shirt collar to reveal a burn.

"They laugh at you," she has told him many times.

"Why shouldn't they laugh?" he asks, arms flapping like a suffering chicken. "*I* laugh at me."

"They call you a fool," she has taunted. "Vishna the Fool."

"Who am I to argue?" This is his answer or a question? She does not know.

"Are you a fool?" she asks.

"Are you?" he returns.

Toba shakes her head no.

"Then you are smart enough to know if I am."

So goes this conversation, as all do—in the crazy circles that moths fly. Toba does not mind the chase. It is an old game. One with rules well learned and honestly abided by, simply because there are none.

It could begin something like this. Toba might say something—a half-thought phrased in a lost tune—and Vishna would turn, sometimes toward her, other times away, and respond to the unspoken question with the other half of a thought, or mention a bit of nonsense or just frown and laugh at the same time, loud and hard, until Toba would join in, not knowing just why, or what was so funny, but confirmed in her uncaring until her aching side would cause her laugh to slow and drip into tears.

But now there is no laughter. Clearly, though perhaps it is not so clear to Vishna, Toba is angry. She is angry with Vishna and her Papa. But if she were forced to choose, it is Vishna with whom she is most angry: for not fighting back, for not caring enough to ask, "Why are you throwing me out of your home, Reb Cohen?" Vishna, if he could hear her thoughts—and she is not certain that he cannot—would say that he could never address Reb Cohen in such a tone. "How could I question a man in his own home? Whatever reason he had for doing what he has done is right under his roof. This is true?"

Toba can offer no answer. But this does not mean she is wrong. Where is it written that no answer means the wrong answer? Nowhere, that's where! And with this proof, her anger soars—almost to the point where she is as disgusted with Vishna as she had been last winter.

He was walking around with a coat of holes. The wool had been a feast for the moths, who left him with nothing but a stained lining to cover his shivering body against the snow and wicked wind of Lenchintz's most unkind months.

"Sell your carvings," Toba had urged as the cure to his running nose, deep cough and aching head. "Then buy yourself a real coat, made of material, from Mr. Kenner. He'll sell you one at such a price it would be a gift."

But did Vishna listen to such good sense? The answer

is easy. Of course not. He had replied to Toba with words so tangled, so slippery that repeating them makes her head spin and her feet lose their grip on the ground. Such phrases could never be retold accurately, of course, but often she has passed down the story to herself alone—no one else would ever believe it—like this:

"I do not sell my carvings because everyone wants them. They say, 'Beautiful, lovely, charming, thank you very much.' And now I can give each one away. If people had to spend their money for them, they would think, 'Oh, maybe I cannot afford this. It is too expensive. What will I have to give up to have it?' And if they don't buy them because they cost too much money, they feel bad. They think, 'It is a shame I cannot earn enough to have the carving.' And what would be worse, just think, if I cannot sell them because they are too expensive, then my carvings will be all around me, worthless. I would get sick of them. I would hate them. Then I would be very sad, as well. And what was before such a joy becomes, with the price, a misery. But now, when I give them away, everyone can afford them, and everyone has them, and there are never enough."

Such is Vishna's masterly power over logic—each sentence an uncharted road, starting out in one direction, turning here, then there, tracking backward, following no signs, leading to who-knows-where. Yet, such a journey with Vishna seems always to bring something fresh, even enough to make a circular path worthwhile. This is what Toba has often said to those who ask why it is she thinks so much of him, why she bothers to waste her time with this man small in size and smaller in mind.

"Enough!" Toba says. "This cannot go on like this."

"If it cannot, then it will not."

"You must not let them push you where they want." She points.

Vishna turns full circle. He does so again, in the opposite direction. "Who is forcing me where?"

"Everyone. My Papa. The whole town!"

Again he spins in both directions, seemingly at once. "The only one I see is you."

Toba stops. There! He does it again, twisting and tangling her until she is bound by her own words. Only a fool could do such a thing. Only a fool.

Toba decides to take another road, her only luggage the hope that this time she will not meet up with herself again.

"Vishna, you told Papa you will marry me."

"As they say, I could do worse."

"It is for my Papa to decide, true?"

"True."

Ah, we agree, she thinks, and makes her next move. "So you will ask him again. This time you will mean it."

"I have always meant it," he says. "But he means what he says, and he says no. Were you not listening?"

"You are impossible!" Toba yells, upset that he's refused the bait.

"So I have heard. Yet here I am, as possible as you, as that toad, as this cane and the stain on my shirt from your momma's wonderful chicken."

"Oh, Vishna," she moans. "What will become of us?"

"Tonight we will sleep and tomorrow we will wake. And further, I cannot even guess."

"No," Toba says.

"No?" He ponders, then brightens. "Of course, you are right. I *can* guess. And my guess is tomorrow we will sleep and tonight we will wake."

"Tomorrow you will ask my Papa to marry me." Toba does not even pause to think, to breathe, to wait for his reaction. Her words are pinpricks, quick, and in their fury each touches Vishna just lightly enough to make him think the ideas are his own. "I will have Momma prepare Papa's favorite meal. Then you will come, after dinner, when he is rested and calm. And I will leave the room, and you will ask him."

Vishna does not answer. He twitches—but not a dancing twitch. His eyes lose their shine and grow dull and solid. His smile draws tight and thin. He leans far, but catches himself, planting his cane firmly.

"You will first tell him how you will care for his youngest. You will find a job. You will sell your carvings. Then you will explain that you are not in much of a position—this you know—but he must understand his Toba is a poor girl herself, from a poor family, and for her to marry the son of a rabbi is little more than a dream. My Papa, of course, will argue. He will say, 'But, Vishna, my Toba is good enough not for the son but for the *rabbi*!' "

Toba's mouth goes chasing after her flying tongue. Her eyes, though, are still, steady on the softening face of the little man.

"You will have to say that you are prepared to accept a modest dowry—perhaps nothing at all—because your position is not one of great wealth. But that your love, you must say, and respect for me—and him, as well—are great and rich."

Toba's probing continues. Deeper go the pricks until Vishna seems to sink back into the shadows. The moon sheds a gold light on the small, hairy man, now looking more beast than human. He hisses at her words, her tiny stabs—how Momma will spit on him for daring to ask to marry her daughter. "She might even throw a pot!" How Papa will tell him he is too old. But he must fight. They will be testing him. Does he love Toba enough to fight for? Enough to make a fool of himself for? He must answer questions such as: Where will they live? How does he think an old man can make a young woman—"a girl," her Papa will no doubt say—happy? What will happen if his carvings do not sell? "For free, yes, they are beautiful, but to reach down in the pocket for them—suddenly the lines and cuts might very well become hideous. What then?"

"You must be prepared to say that you will work three—four—jobs to make sure I am cared for. And you must tell my Papa what Toba means to you. How you will die for her. How you are not worth even the wood you carve without her. How you will be cursed the rest of your days without Toba as your wife."

Never before has Toba seen Vishna so still. He is like one of his carvings. Rigid, yet moving, smooth, yet angled. Crafted by her coldly aimed cuts. But for what reason? She couldn't possibly want Vishna for her husband—though when she was younger, she would think such thoughts. And here she is—fourteen, while girls of twelve are married. Could she possibly be an old maid? Is Vishna her savior? Could Vishna be the one for her? In the pause of confusion, she can already see him beginning to move.

"And you won't give up your fight, your asking for my hand," she continues, pointing, her eyes squinting tight, warning, "until Papa agrees. You will not walk away from him until he embraces you and calls you 'my son.' You will toast with fine schnapps to our long, healthy lives together and the birth of our son—his grandson."

With each word, Toba cuts, carves, paints, onto the

blank canvas of Vishna. To capture Vishna himself, as she might a deer or a house or a child in a painting, is impossible. To do that she must understand the subject. How can she possibly know what is going on in the dark, muddy mind of Vishna? No, painting Vishna cannot be done—his expressions do not hold still. They slide and fade into one another as if he hasn't any bones beneath his skin. Even when he seems to be barely moving, Toba notices the small changes, the gentle movements like the final ripples in a lake after the stone has sunk deep and settled on the bottom.

"Vishna will ask Toba to be his wife?" The voice is loud and startled, as if the thought had just occurred to him while he was alone, not thinking of anything in particular. A new idea; a coin freshly found in the dirt. Toba waits for him to answer his own question. "I should walk up to Reb Cohen and speak to him." Vishna bows his head. "I will say, 'Reb Cohen, sir, I would like to have your youngest to be my bride.' " He bobs his head, turns this way and that, then a way that Toba was certain could not be done.

"I will get a job, Reb Cohen," he acts out, taking his hat from his balding head in pantomine, for he rarely wears a hat. "I will care for her, respect her, treasure her, Reb Cohen. My oath."

Toba must take a quick step back as Vishna performs. His gestures are wild as he points with a directness that surprises her, then follows with a sorrowful look turned into one of great intent. He bends his crooked leg, almost pleading. He straightens tall (tall for Vishna) and looks her imagined Papa straight in his blind eyes.

"Yes, of course I understand, sir," Vishna nods, his eyes now closed, painfully listening to the silent voice of Toba's Papa. "What you say is true. Every word clear as water. A wife is a man's most honored possession. Yet, still, as it says in the Torah, she is not his to possess. Such wisdom. And so I will tend to this treasure. Be her owner and be owned by her. Yes, yes. A promise, Reb Cohen. May God's ears be open to swallow my oath. May His pen write each word to prove Vishna a liar."

Toba is enraptured by the scene. She can see her Papa: watches him consider; hears his thoughtful words, slow and feeling; even smells his rich, warm scent.

"Another truth, Reb Cohen! Though from your mouth it comes as no surprise." Vishna bows, mournfully, beaten. "I am a beggar. A poor man. I take my meals at the kindness of my neighbors. I have no work. And you are right in your concern as to your daughter's future. 'How will she eat?' you are right to ask. How will we feed the mouths of our children?"

It is so like Toba's Papa to think not only of today, but of tomorrow. It is his deep love that takes his mind from what quickly sparkles and soon fades to what may be dark yet lasting.

"But I will work. I will work hard, Reb Cohen. If I cannot tend to your daughter, my Toba, in the way you see proper, I will return her to you and never be seen in my beloved Lenchintz again. Never."

There is a silence that Toba dares not disturb. Tears mark Vishna's face. She can see the same tears in her Papa's eyes. Vishna takes the cane from his right hand, puts it into his left and reaches out to shake with her Papa. But her Papa cannot see the hand. He opens his heavy arms, his sad arms, and like a wounded child, a grateful Vishna rushes, stumbles in.

"It is a match! So it will be! Vishna will take Toba as his bride!"

Vishna shouts wildly, his voice tripping higher, like a caged bird set free. With speed that seems even to amaze himself, he turns and, as if the wind has picked him up, rises into flight, twitching, cackling, cane waving, down the road into the darkness, leaving Toba behind, lost and alone outside the house where she was born.

Two days later, the uneasy feeling still wandering within her, everything becomes clear with five hard knocks on the door.

"Reb Cohen, I know that it is not my night to take a meal with you and your family but, please, I would like to—no, I *must*—have a word with you. Please."

Toba, now struggling to lose herself, cannot. Her Papa offers Vishna a chair. Momma takes a plate from the cupboard, though dinner has been served and Toba is certain that there is not even a bone left in the pot.

"You will eat, Vishna," Momma orders, setting down the plate.

"No, please, no, I cannot. Already I have had two dinners; the first with Mrs. Lendle—a cook, she isn't. The second was with Mr. Berman—the widower. He, on the other hand, can make a skinny bird taste fat and moist. Thank you."

All this polite talk is torture to Toba's ears. Her breath is tight in her throat. She needs a swallow of water but does not have the nerve to stand.

"You have come to talk, Vishna. Then I will listen." Papa lifts himself from the chair and, turning, reaches out his arm, which folds around Vishna's bony shoulders, and the small man, known as the fool of Lenchintz, guides them both into the darkness of Papa's workroom.

"What could be so important for Vishna to talk about?" Momma asks, taking the clean plate from the table and washing it before she replaces it in the cupboard. "He's never said no to one of my meals before." Toba does not answer, but stares at the bottom of the closed door for a crack of light which never appears.

"He is a man," Momma continues. "This is difficult to remember. And a man must have his word. True?" She answers her own question with a pause. "Even Vishna needs to be heard as a man."

The words hit against Toba's ears like a slap to the

head. She stings with guilt, and is dizzy with terror that what was the other night a game between boy and girl is now a battle between two men.

I was just teasing him, she thinks, the way I always do, just seeing if he'd obey or fight back. Like a stray dog one pokes with a stick.

"So, what do you have to say for yourself, quiet one?" Momma passes Toba, touching her daughter's shoulder. "You are a woman, after all. Like a man, a woman must have her word. Though God knows it must be a quieter word and more often than not, a prayer."

Again Toba is struck—now with a dull blow.

"You are a woman, after all." She hears her Momma's voice echo. Toba can remember the times she has insisted that she was just that—a woman. Times not long enough ago to call the past, but Momma's only repsonse had been, "Of course you are, my darling," or, "I am not yet ready to give you up."

And now, in a moment, Vishna the Fool has grown to be a man and Toba the Child has become a woman. And This Man is in her Papa's dark room, asking for This Woman's hand in marriage.

It is natural enough. A man finds a woman. He needs a wife, of course. And she a husband. So why not? These are the thoughts of a heartsick newborn woman.

"So it is," her Momma sighs, releasing her daughter's shoulder. "You do not feel like talking. This, too, is a woman's choice—oftentimes it is the choice of a wise woman. You are a wise woman, Toba Cohen. Of course, this is natural. Look from whom you were born."

Toba the woman. Toba the wise. Toba the wife of Vishna. Toba the wife of a fool. Toba the fool.

The door opens. There is only darkness. And silence. Momma stops her cleaning. Toba closes her eyes. She prays her silent, womanly prayer.

The sound of footsteps forces open her lids. Toba sees only Vishna come from the room. He is not smiling. Nor is he frowning. With Vishna, though, either sign would lead her nowhere. He wiggles, coughs, taps his cane, as he makes his way to the front door. Just as he reaches his destination, he turns and quickly makes his way back to the dark room. For what? A final word? To plead his case one last time? To thank Toba's Papa—*his* Papa—once again? No, to close the door to the workroom shut. What can this mean? Vishna's face reveals nothing. It is as blank as a human face can be. At the door again, he bows once to Momma and then, pausing, as if he wants to say something but cannot, again bows quickly toward Toba and is out the door.

Toba does not see her Papa this night. He remains in his dark workroom. It is all she can do to stop herself from running in and throwing herself into his arms to cry and cry. But Momma, who has once already asked him what the matter was with Vishna, has received no answer and so warned Toba that she would not be told good night this night by her Papa.

Toba's dream is of a photograph. Framed on a table, it pictures Vishna and herself on the day of their wedding. They are in the woods, not in shul or a house. They are not wearing wedding gowns but regular clothes, perhaps rags. Just where the table is on which the photograph sits, Toba does not know. Something else that she does not know is whether or not she is happy. Or even if Vishna is happy. The two are like his carvings—still, unmoving and unreal.

She hears her name. Toba wakes and sees the photograph on the table; still she doesn't know where she is. Her Papa is over her.

"Toba. Toba, what is to be?"

Toba looks up through her sleep-clouded vision. Is she still dreaming?

"Toba, he comes for your hand. He wants to marry you. He says that I should not be so prideful. That he is an honest man. He tells me that you love him. These are *your* words, he says. He says you want him as your husband."

Toba can see by the faded light from her window and the cold that creeps in the air that it is more night than morning. Her Papa looks gray in the weak light. His beard seems to float down like a stream from his face to his feet. He looks much the way she has imagined God.

"Toba, what have you done? What have you done, Toba?"

Toba reaches out from her bed, from her sleep, and

hugs her Papa. She can feel his strength and his breath warm on her neck. She hears that she is not the only one crying. He moans and trembles. Even at the saddest times, when her Papa's sister passed on, he did not act so. Toba pulls from his arms, now thin and weak, and sees that it is not her Papa at all who is weeping. It is Vishna. He smiles kindly at her, his red eyes swollen and dancing, his lips bitten and bloody, his fingers, like twigs in a storm, disjointed and dangling . . .

This is Toba's dream.

"Such a dream," Momma would say if Toba were to confide in her. "It is a sign of things to come. This I can tell you."

Toba is afraid even to think what such "things" are.

Her mind clearer than most mornings, her heart more troubled, Toba makes her way slowly down the stairs. The sounds of breakfast are a warning. Quietly she sits, listening to her Momma list the chores she must perform "all before lunch." Papa listens, his hands folded around a glass of tea that is more steam than brew. He bows and breathes deeply the dark color and lemon scent.

Momma brings Toba her tea and a thick slice of warm bread with the butter well melted. The cereal is in need of some stirring yet.

It seems like just another morning, Toba says to herself—right now her only sure friend. The same quietness of tone in conversation. The same short sentences with little hints of sleep between. The same taste to the bread and tea. Could she have dreamed everything? Even her scene with Vishna?

"I had a dream," Toba says, testing.

"A dream?" Momma asks from over the stove.

Now the question becomes which dream to tell. The one that remains in her head like a fever after the sickness has been cured, or the one that Toba could well have imagined during a storming night—the dream that would be a plea for help? How she wants to apologize, to find out what was said and heard in the dark of her Papa's room last night between him and Vishna. How many times she has relied on the sharp, caring eyes and ears of her parents to admit her wrongs for her . . . If she lied, and days later was still uncaught—leaving Toba even more guilty—a confession would force itself from her, a half truth in a dimly-lit dream. Momma or Papa, sometimes both, would finish this dream, understanding what was before unclear, or perhaps what they have always known, and everything would be settled.

"I, too, had a dream last night," her Papa says.

Toba sighs easily. Again, she is saved. Now he will paint his own picture for them. It may be long and involved like a midrash from the Talmud, a story that has a beginning and ending, but the middle can only be caught by the quick and knowing eye of wisdom.

"Papa, you had a dream!" Momma stops stirring the cereal and comes over to the table, her hands wringing. "You did not tell me?"

"But it is not what is in our heads while we sleep that we should discuss here. I am right, Toba?"

There is no question in his voice.

"It is not a dream when a man comes into your house, opens his heart and asks to marry your daughter."

Momma gasps.

"This is what happens when we are awake and living," he continues. Momma reaches out for the rag on the stove and puts it to her face. There is nothing that Toba can hide behind, nowhere to turn, no half-truth to tell.

"This is not a dream. It is not another of your games. You understand, Toba?"

Again, no question. And no answer. Now she understands that no answer makes it the wrong answer.

"I could give my blessing, of course. And it would be a match. There would be nothing else to be done. It could not be undone. It is my word. You know the importance of our words, Toba? I will give my word and you in the same breath if this is what you want."

"My baby . . ." The rag cannot swallow Momma's sobs. "A nothing . . ."

Yesterday, a girl. Last night, a woman. This morning, a baby.

Toba stands and quickly—trying to outstep her thoughts—walks to the door and leaves. She has only been to Vishna's house in the woods twice before—once when she was young and with Anna and Bella. He was sick with the illness that had left him crippled. The second time involved one of her lies. She was waiting for Vishna and he did not come. Momma said he would come soon, but he did not. Toba asked if she could go to his house, explaining that she knew the way and was only going to make sure Vishna did not come down with another illness. She remembers Momma making excuses. "Vishna does not have a chair for people to sit on" was one. Another was, "You cannot go to Vishna because he is not there. He is on his way here. You will miss each other." Toba had waited another impatient hour, and then sneaked away from the house while Momma was in the back, hanging laundry. And when she returned, prepared to tell Momma that she had met Vishna down the road and they had gone off together, she saw the lie would not work. There was Momma on the porch, and beside her, half standing, half leaning, was Vishna. Toba had quickly made up some story about a friend that she'd made and stayed with for a while, then artfully turned to Vishna and redirected the blame. "Where were you, Vishna? I was waiting and waiting!"

If that moment showed anything about Toba's and Vishna's relationship, it is this. That one could be here and the other could be there, yet they were together. It may not make sense, Toba would agree, but then again, just because something makes sense does not mean it is proof of anything.

It is this abandonment of logic that is of most important when dealing with Vishna. If you forego reason, then it becomes obvious he is not the fool others think. But now, as she makes her steps brisk and light, Toba wonders why such a natural thing as this should suddenly be a problem? Why, after a lifetime of living in a world that they created, a place with no doors or locks to insure their privacy, should such a place seem so foreign?

The thought of her separate world takes Toba to another world. No more than a hundred steps from her home, she wonders why it is that her Momma does not come out and yell for her to come back. She must know where she is going. There is a loneliness in this thought. A feeling she has left something behind, something that she can never again go back for. Or maybe it is a feeling that she herself has been passed by, left behind.

Turning from the thought and the house, Toba aims her steps and mind toward Vishna. Her memory serves as her guide and performs well. It is only minutes before she is on the well-beaten path into the woods known as Sobosinski's Forest, after a family of hermits who once—and perhaps still—lived there.

Toba imagines the path before her as the aisle of a shul—the wedding aisle. But now she must walk it alone. She begins, and is stopped by a tree, wet with small drops of sap. Toba reaches out her hand, touches her finger to the sticky syrup, and puts the sweetness to her lips. "The kiss of spring." This is what Bella would call the tree's juice. The taste, blending with the words she has not heard in years, takes Toba back a long way. She pictures in her mind the three of them—Anna, Bella and Toba—playing, teasing. In her mind she hears their singing, the three voices so different, rising and joining. A sound she has not shared in too long a time.

A bird calls high and clear. Toba turns to see Vishna's house—a shack of rotten wood, discarded coats, clothing he has gathered from the trash, pieces donated by the people of Lenchintz. There is a dress of Momma's. It is the one Momma never liked very much, worn only when she cleaned the floors. Toba can see, even from such a distance, the patches at the knees. Now it is a doormat, proud and unashamed. A laugh escapes wild from Toba's serious face.

"What will I tell him?" she asks the kind tree, which offers more kisses but not a single word of hope. Now Toba knows for sure that no answer means the wrong answer.

"You must understand, Vishna, it is all a game," Toba sighs, her eyes large, pleading with a childish sorrow. "I *do* love you. This is the truth. But what you heard was a dream. Yes, a dream painted in our sleeps. And, like a dream, it fooled us. Pitiful us!" She forces a laugh, but her voice again breaks to reveal her weakness. "Our marriage cannot be."

Toba imagines the strength that had magically appeared, the strength that had filled Vishna just nights before, now bleed away. She sees a powerful man shrink, sees his broad chest shrivel, the shine of his eyes dim, his hands lose their nerve. How proud he had been! She can still hear his voice commanding her Papa. The courage he showed, the compassion, the wisdom. Yes! At that moment she would have married him.

"Just a dream—a dream we breathed together," Toba continues, struggling for her words, for her strength, her courage. "A beautiful dream of Vishna and Toba married."

It is useless. Her words are empty. This is the difference between them. Vishna's are honest tales—so they are real. This is why he could make her believe her Papa was standing before her, crying, pondering, laughing, when he was not there at all. This is why Vishna can be who he is forever. Because he is a believer. But what does she offer? Nothing but lies, selfish, mean and cowardly. Lies even she does not believe. And now she is about to make her lies truths by lying even further. And what is worse, what is as vicious as it is true, is that Toba knows that Vishna, the believer, will trust her, will nod his deformed head and mumble, "Of course, yes, no doubt," even before she speaks her first false word. Perhaps this is why she has lied to him before—for the same reason she has looked after him while others have laughed, been his good friend when they called him names. Because he *is* a fool. Because she is not a fool. She is not a fool. This she must believe. Even if it is another of her lies, this she must believe.

Now, Toba steps strongly toward Vishna's house. It

is with the same certainty that she knocks on the door. "I will tell him plainly that I am a liar. That he deserves better. That I am not worthy. I will humble myself. I will apologize."

From behind her, Toba feels a poke at her side. Quickly she turns. Vishna stands, leans, twitches as he always has, his cane swinging above the ground, his laugh tripping higher, his eyes crazy.

"Oh, Vishna," Toba hears herself cry. "Am I a fool? Am I a fool?"

"Of course not," he says, and deftly wipes a tear from her cheek. "Would Vishna marry a fool?"

The Mirror

Charming is something Toba has been called often—more often than she has been called trustworthy, adoring and, yes, more often than she has been called beautiful. She would have it no other way, though she would not argue with a few more *beautifuls*.

Charm is a talent, a language, a tool. To Toba it is, above all, a mirror. This mirror is not one made of glass, nor is it crafted with a fancy silver frame. It does not even have a handle, yet Toba knows how to handle this mirror well, and she does so, often.

This mirror is always with Toba, which makes perfect sense. Would a cobbler be without his nails, a musician without his instruments, a beggar without his hat in his hands? But even more odd than the fact that Toba's mirror is not made of glass is the fact that with all its use, Toba has never once viewed her reflection in this piece. No, this mirror is solely for the eyes of others.

Perhaps this may sound like a riddle. It is not. More, it is a mystery, one which Toba has not had to work to master.

A simple display of her prowess could be witnessed on any odd day and go perfectly unnoticed. But then this is a compliment to Toba's art. For there is great beauty in the workings of the miraculous, and even more so when the miracle is performed without the slightest show of strain. After all, who would trust a dentist with hands that shake or a baker who must pause to ponder just how much yeast goes into his challah?

Such a performance could go like this.

"Oh, Toba, how are you, darling?" Mrs. Litvin might say, seeing Toba is fine. "If you would like to know how I am, I must tell you that my packages"—she pauses to catch her laboring breaths—"are too heavy for these old arms."

Toba can see that the woman is not lying, though she is in part acting—there is little reason for her to whimper as she does. And so it is here that Toba's mirror, her charm, can be most helpful.

"But, Mrs. Litvin," Toba might very well say—almost sing—stepping just close enough to the packages so that she could either take them herself or just as easily lean on them. "I have no doubt that your groceries are heavy, but do not think about them as they are. No, no, think about what a tasty, light meal you will make from them!"

Mrs. Litvin swallows her whimpers and begins to straighten.

"Why, you, of all the cooks in Lenchintz and who knows how much further away, are known for biscuits that float like clouds, for meat so delicately spiced the tongue is delighted into a dance!"

"Oh, Toba Cohen!" Mrs. Litvin would say—in fact, many times has said—her arms truly feeling new strength, her packages wondrously uplifted. "You know, it is a secret—my recipe for biscuits. I would tell you, but then, what would poor little Mrs. Litvin be known for? You understand, of course."

Toba nods, understanding that Mrs. Litvin's biscuits have been said to be the perfect patches for leaky roofs. But why mention something like that? There is no good reason to have the woman believe anything but that her biscuits are heaven-scented. If she chooses to think such thoughts as she merrily goes on her way, the bundles in her arms a joy, Toba is not one to get in her way.

Now, Toba could easily have turned and walked away when she saw the woman trudging up the hill. She could have played deaf to the sound of her name. These actions would have done the job of freeing her from carrying the woman's load, but they would also have been considered rude. And from such rudeness, especially in the village of Lenchintz, comes talk. And when people talk, Toba knows, you can be certain that what they are going to say will not be nice. And what good ever came from such words—especially if you are the person they are speaking poorly of, especially if what they are saying is true?

So, instead of being rude, Toba is pleasant. Instead of blocked ears, she opens them to hear the person's every word, complaint, question and, eventually—because she *is* so pleasant—compliment. And instead of walking away, she walks straight toward them, smiling. And they are so pleased to be greeted in such a fashion that they are satisfied to walk away—though they had wanted something from Toba—with nothing. Or, in Mrs. Litvin's case, with everything.

This is quite simply and accurately how Toba's charm works. But it is what is behind the mirror that Toba has really mastered. For there is really nothing so astounding that one would stop what he was doing to witness someone being nice to another instead of being cruel. As it was written, "Do unto others . . ." What is really at the heart here is the angle, the measure, the flair, with which Toba works her charm. For example, Mrs. Litvin, the poor dear, took down a deep breath and went briskly along with her load as if she were carrying a bagful of dreams. But what would have happened had Toba said other words to her—words such as, "Mrs. Litvin, it is true that your bundle is heavy but soon you will be in your home and your weak arms will enjoy the rest they have earned," instead of what she said about the "light meal"? Either way she would have to be considered pleasant or nice, or any other like-minded phrase, and yet, had she said those words, the effect, the reaction, the reflection, would have been altogether different. This is the glint, the sparkle, the art, in Toba's mirror.

She knows well Mrs. Litvin's desire, jealous and stubborn, to be a highly praised cook. The fairs that each spring attract the finest bakers, jam makers, picklers, with their challenges for prizes, have always left Mrs. Litvin wanting. She so much wants to be seen in a good light. Well, Toba does just that. The magic of her glassless mirror catches the light that Mrs. Litvin so desires—not the light of the sun or the moon or the candle's flame—but the invisible light the mind casts. It is in this fine glow that the poor baker in Mrs. Litvin becomes a prize-winning chef. Simply by listening to Toba's rhythmic tone, her precise words, and studying her graceful movements, one can actually see—believe!—what one most wants. The ugly are given handsome faces, the wonderers have their deepest questions answered, travelers are firmly, safely rooted.

Such are the profits of Toba's charm. Honest they may not be considered in the Book of Laws, yet she could convincingly argue that there is really no harm done. And should it come before a court—and should she find herself losing her case—Toba has the knowledge that she could always charm the judge into seeing it her way. "Your

Honor, it is plainly a way I have created to make not only mine but everyone's days easier, more pleasant, more enjoyable." And who could argue with that? Just a little grease put to the wheel in order to keep things in motion and stop that awful screeching.

"Toba, you are so kind. So wise. So charming!" Mrs. Litvin would say, nodding, pondering the thought of her meat, so juicy it bathes in its natural gravy. And Toba would nod just as thoughtfully, admiring her work, seeing the great pleasure, the gentle serenity, on the woman's face where only moments before was sweat and wrinkled pain. What's more, she can watch Mrs. Litvin take one step, then another, her bundle not one ounce lighter, though she carries it like the air carries a summer's song. But most important is that Toba can walk away, herself empty-handed, her arms free as the words that will soon float from her tongue, seeing Mr. Kelpermeyer stuck at the roadside with his lame mule.

The Mikvah

In the mikvah, Toba has heard, one whispers, because God's ear is close. She does not know if this is true, but she has seen the faces of the women returning from the house with the stream running through. They walk—some in groups, others alone—slowly, free, arms swinging, faces lighted.

Each month when Momma comes back, there is an easiness even in her hurried steps, as if the water has seeped through her thick skin and on it floats her spirit.

Toba will be going to the mikvah today, but she will not be going to the one in Lenchintz. And though it is custom, her first time will not be witnessed by all the women in the Cohen family. She will be alone, except for Momma.

When Toba first heard the plan, two nights ago, Momma had hushed the words that told what was to be. Toba understood without question and, though frightened, she had fallen asleep with the feeling that the mikvah was a serious and beautiful ritual.

"This is not for any other ears," Momma warned before she had closed the door. "Not even your Papa's."

Again Toba understood without explanation.

The reason she cannot tell anyone is the same reason she is not going to the mikvah of Lenchintz. Toba should not be going to the mikvah at all.

Only women who are married or engaged to be wed are allowed in the mikvah. It is here they are cleansed before God for their husbands. By entering the mikvah, Toba is not only going against what is custom, but she is breaking the law of the Torah. By bringing Toba into the mikvah, Momma is committing a sin.

"So you will be cleansed before God now and later, too, when it will be time for your husband. To be too clean is a sin we can live with," is how Momma settled the matter.

They are going to the mikvah because Toba will be leaving soon for America. The mikvah is a precaution, or perhaps it is a cure; Toba can see both sides. After all, who knows for sure if there are such things as mikvahs in America? Who knows even if God is there? So they have decided to break the laws in order to keep their faith. Although these could have been the actual words Momma used to explain the confused matter, they are not. They are Toba's silent words—again not needing the air of voice to give them meaning or truth. Toba understands the delicate balance of idea and feeling, just as she understands that when they lie to Papa, telling him they are going to Gez to find a good, strong trunk for Toba to make certain everything arrives well, they are telling a lie to keep the truth.

Gez is far enough that Toba and Momma can begin their journey early, before the neighbors wake and ask questions. The horse and carriage rented from Mr. Kelmer must keep a brisk pace and must be trusted not to reveal anything seen or heard on the secret sojourn.

"Now, Toba, this is a very sacred covenant the Jewish woman must fulfill. The mikvah is an obligation. It is a blessing." These are the serious words Toba expected from Momma. Thoughts she imagined all mommas pass down to their daughters at such a time.

"Such a pleasant day. I think we should take back a little something special for dinner tonight, since we will be in Gez. What do you think?" are the words actually said.

This is a trick, of course—quickly spotted by a wise Toba—a trick to take her mind from what is about to happen. It is something Momma has done with great success since her daughters were babies to ease the pain of a fall, sweeten bad dreams and scare off fears the night would bring.

Toba plays along.

"Almonds," she suggests, naming a sweet she knows is out of season. "Papa has been asking for them. We should bring back almonds."

Momma takes her gaze from the soft red dirt road to wink at her daughter, realizing Toba knows just what is happening.

"Almonds," she says, pleased.

About a mile or so from the mikvah, their chatter fades. And once on the road that leads to just one place, the quiet is only disturbed by the whisper of the river.

The mikvah of Gez is much larger than the one in Lenchintz. It stands on the river, wide, solid and severe, though it offers a lightness with its wide-angled roof and fresh coat of white paint. The sparkling water runs lively from the great, dark western passageway and out through the smaller eastern gate.

Once they step down from the carriage, Momma never leaves Toba's side—always touching her, playing with her hair, smoothing her forehead, fixing her ruffled dress, silently reminding Toba of their bond now, forever.

Inside the mikvah, they are greeted by a large woman, who looks at Toba and nods often—the way doctors do before giving you something awful to swallow—her eyes full of that knowing shine and syrupy kindness, which Toba takes as a warning.

"It's been seven days since," Momma nods sternly.

The woman looks away from Toba, her face changing weather to dark business.

"Her first time?" She purses her lips, nodding her head up and down, slowly, not waiting for an answer. "The wedding is . . . ?"

"Three nights," Momma sighs, bothered, trying to hurry such questions.

"The groom's full name here." The woman looks over again to Toba while turning the large, flat book around so Momma can fill in the information.

Whose name could she put down? Toba wonders.

"And the rabbi who will perform the ceremony, here." The woman points without looking.

She is going to lie about a rabbi's name! Toba shouts to herself.

With unflinching determination, Momma completes the form, signing her name at the bottom with a bold stroke. Then, with a look of great sternness, she hands the pencil to Toba and points where she should sign.

The fat woman surveys the information carefully, mouthing each word with the suspicious air of a policeman who can sense the robber close by.

"Ah, he is a fine rabbi!" The woman nods, impressed, touching the hair from her chin. "My sister, Rachel, was also married by him. So, tell me, who is the cantor?"

Toba looks away.

"Listen, we do not have time," Momma answers, waving the fee in front of the woman's face.

The money is exchanged. The door is opened. And Toba, with her Momma not leading, not following—so it is impossible to tell who this mikvah is for—enters the candle-lit room of the ritual bath.

You go into the room. You take off your clothing. You step into the water. You say the prayer. Then you come out of the water.

This is what Toba had told herself she would do in the mikvah. And she is right, except for one thing. The feeling. The ghostly aura that rises with her—on her—as she steps from the water. It is as if the water which was supposed to carry the dirt from her now leaves her with something. What, she cannot say. Such a feeling cannot be compared to anything else she's ever experienced, heard of or even dreamed. She doubts that such a feeling even has a name.

When she is told to take her clothes off by the large woman wearing a solid green smock—not the first large woman but another one, even larger—Toba, knowing this was going to be necessary, still feels the uneasiness she'd thought she'd feel. But because she cannot think of another way of getting from where she stands to the water without the protection of clothes—as she had planned—she frowns and surrenders her nakedness to the eyes of the stranger.

First, her feet are scrubbed, each of her nails, then her legs, with a brush whose bristles look soft and white but feel like a wire used to clean burnt pots. The red marks are proof of the large woman's strength, Toba's silence is proof of her willingness to endure the pain of this frightening tradition.

As she works Toba over, the woman hums a song. To Toba it sounds much like a song of war, with its great pounding rises and solid rhythm. Toba wonders if this is the song of the mikvah. A song of war as they prepare another warrior. But what could she be fighting for? Toba questions while the woman scrubs her skin as if she is grooming an animal. When she cannot solve the puzzle, Toba proceeds to another thought: how the only other woman to ever bathe her in such a manner was her Momma.

When the woman's hands rise up the leg, higher than the thigh, Toba shudders and fights to chase her mind far away. Her eyes, like spears, aim for the walls of the mikvah. In the candlelight, she is still able to see the tile pieces, tiny specks of seashell, rock and smoothed stone—different sizes and colors and shapes pieced together—all showing scenes of the Torah—all having to do with water. There is the basket carrying Moses down the Nile. There is the Great Flood that rained forty days and forty nights. And on the storm's river floats Noah's Ark, guided by the white dove with the olive branch of hope in its beak. There is an older Moses—arms outstretched—parting the Red Sea; the pools of water turning to blood from one of the plagues on Pharaoh's Egypt. And there is the scene of the mikvah: women standing in stone pools, their bodies wet and peaceful as they clean themselves in the fine light of the moon.

Now, perhaps for the first time, Toba sees the simple beauty in this tradition. And as she searches further into the murals, she can see in the shining tiles and gentle water below, the reflection of the woman combing straight her long, dark hair.

When the scrubbing stops, Toba, as though she's been carrying a great weight for miles, gives way under the sudden easing of pressure. Her knees weaken and she nearly faints.

"Stand!" the woman orders without even reaching out. Toba responds to the order like a soldier, conquering her legs. She does not have to look to know her Momma is staring hard at her, willing her strength.

"Now, Toba, you will step down into the water and dip yourself so your head and hair are fully under. Then you will rise up and recite the prayer over The Dipping. Then down you will go six more times. Each time your head must come up out of the water, then go down under. No part of you is to be dry. And remember not to touch anything—not the wood around you or the tiles—and your fingers, they are to be spread to let the water run through the body's every path."

Toba nods at each instruction.

"Remember why it is you are here. You are not taking a bath for a party, yes? You are here for your husband. When you are under the water, your thoughts must be on this so you clean the mind as well. From your mouth to God's ear."

Toba stops her nodding when the woman speaks of the reason she is there. There is no husband. God must know this. She cannot fool Him, not when He is so close. So she turns and walks down into the water, thinking that the ocean will be her husband. The ocean which she will cross to America will care for her, provide for her.

When she comes up the first time, Toba looks to see her Momma. Her eyes—because she did not want to close them—are full of water. She can see that this is also true for Momma. As she hushes the words of the prayer, Momma silently mouths the words with her.

"Mazel tov, darling. Mazel tov." The woman with the strong hands and the war song now gently dries Toba with a towel so soft it tickles. It is impossible to believe that these are the same hands that pushed and prodded Toba as if she were a piece of meat at the butcher's. "You are all right," she croons. "Now you are kosher." She goes on, but now it is Toba who does not feel the need to speak. This does not come from the uneasiness of her nakedness. It is something else.

From a bag older than Toba herself, Momma takes out new clothes, wrapped in paper. Toba takes the gifts piece by piece. The starchy newness feels strange to her body, and when she walks out of the mikvah's damp yellow glow into the front room, she passes the fat woman with the ledger, sure she will not recognize her. But even through the different clothes, the woman tells Toba she remembers her with a look that says, "So now you, too, know."

Momma does not say a word as they walk to the carriage. From her bag she pulls out two sweets. One she hands to Toba with a force that says, "Eat."

Toba obeys, thinking, how odd: a candy at this time. She would expect—demand!—a candy when she was a child coming from the doctor, but this is not necessary any longer. Has she not just proven this?

With a hard crack, Toba bites into the shell of the sweet, letting the sugary syrup flood her mouth, washing over her tongue.

"Sweetness for your life," Momma sighs deeply. "Sweetness for all your life." She cries, and now Toba is flooded not only from the inside but outside as well, with Momma's great hugs, bringing Toba to her, rocking them both. "Sweetness for your voyage," she hushes into Toba's ear. "Sweetness for your children."

It is some time, but when there are no tears left, the women turn to fulfill their journey. Having whispered into the ear of God, they pray that He might now look the other way.

At the Hands of a Thief

Toba is a spy. Bent and half-hidden behind a thick, moving crowd, she watches him again reach out from under an old woman's package and steal an apple from the fruit cart. Then, with the sharp movements of a cat, he turns and coolly walks off to the baker's corner. This time, he stands with his back to the wares. The baker is making change. If it weren't for Toba's quick eye, she would not catch his hand rise from the vent of his coat and lift two—three!—cakes without breaking off a crumb. He feeds his already stuffed pockets and calmly moves on. Toba follows the thief until he has either no more pockets to fill, has picked and chosen from every cart in the market or just cannot find anything else that seems appealing.

This thief is no one Toba has ever seen before, nor does he resemble anyone she knows. So it is probably true that he has no family in Lenchintz. His overcoat, which is too long and big for him—and would usually be unnecessary on this summer morning—either hides his fat or conceals his thinness. In fact, it is difficult to tell almost anything about him. From where she is, now moving so as not to lose him in the crowd, Toba can barely make out his dark eyes, his nose straight and narrow, and his square chin. She tries to memorize his every feature so she can answer the police's detailed questions. Perhaps the only one she will not be able to answer with any certainty is just why she continues to follow him as his smooth strides take him quickly from the scene of the crime.

When they are far enough from the market that Toba can no longer hear the fishwoman call out this morning's fresh catch or the basket weaver's constant arguing over prices, Toba stops. "This is foolishness," she scolds herself. But her curiosity blocks her ears, and commands her timid legs deeper into the woods after the thief. When she finds him her curiosity is teased that much more. Oddly posed on his toes, nearly pressed up against a young tree, the thief observes a worm, a moth, a butterfly—at such a distance, Toba cannot say for sure just what has captured his attention.

"I saw you steal that food!" Toba calls, then quickly

sneaks behind a large, green bush whose leaves tremble with dew. Slowly, he turns about, and as if he's always known just where she was, his eyes, like arrows, find and pierce her.

"I did not steal this food," he says, standing in place, reaching into his pocket and showing an apple. "I paid for it. I *worked* for it. Stealing, as I am sure you witnessed, is very hard work." He lifts the apple high to make his point. "This is the *fruit* of my labor."

He takes a step toward the bush, and smiles a shining, clean smile. Toba thinks he might be younger than she'd first thought.

"As it says in Genesis, 'Man shall earn his food by the sweat of his brow.' "

He takes another step toward Toba, making it impossible for her to believe that he does not see her perfectly.

"And you know what the rabbis say about this—the fruits born of hard labor?" He waits, though Toba does not reply. "They say they are no sweeter than the fruits the rich man eats for not toiling at all." He laughs hard. Too hard. This frightens Toba. And when he bites deeply, angrily into the apple, the cracking sound nearly causes her to cry.

"So now that you know me so well, aren't you going to come out from behind that bush?" he asks, that laugh clear in his voice. "You look, I must be honest, quite foolish."

The word "foolish," like a whip to her back, snaps Toba straight up.

"Well!" he sighs. "That is somewhat better. At least I can see your dirty face." He takes very quick steps toward her. Toba retreats, but he is too fast. His hands—those magical hands—reach out and steal a pinch from her cheek. Toba recoils, her hand to her face, yet she cannot help but wonder at how soft those terrible hands are.

"Shy?" He is amused, and takes another hard bite of his apple, nearly finishing it. "I wouldn't think one who follows a stranger out into the woods alone would be the sort to be timid." He spins and walks off, pondering his question. He turns back, quick as a snake. "Or perhaps it is an act. A trap you village girls weave to capture poor innocents such as myself." Again he laughs, deep, making Toba rethink her guess at his age. His teeth give off a cold, white shine.

"I have no intention of 'trapping' you," Toba repeats his word, her voice sharp with disdain.

"Then, tell me, my spider, why did you follow me?" He now steps to the side, one foot over the other, and kicks the core of his chewed apple high, away. "Did you want my fruit?" He pulls another apple from his pocket and holds it out toward her. "Is this what you want? To steal my fruit? You do not have to steal it from me. Here, I will give it to you free. No?" He bites into this one as he did the other. The skin cracks and bursts with juice. "I have had better," he says, letting the juice drip down his chin.

What are you doing, Toba? Have you lost your mind? I send you down for a few items and this is what you do? What happens is your own fault. I cannot look after you forever, the voice of her Momma, of anyone with any sense, warns in Toba's head.

"Your name is . . ." He turns again, this time closing his eyes, putting the apple to his nose, inhaling deeply. ". . . Sadie. No, Margaret. No, let me see, ahh . . ." He stops his spinning, opens his eyes and sighs, "You have me."

"Toba." She hears herself speak with a giggle, but then quickly realizes she has been tricked. You should know better than to give away anything—even your name—especially to a thief, she scolds herself, knowing with each unbalanced moment that following him here was a terrible mistake.

"*Toba?*" he considers, tastes as if her name were another apple he has stolen. "Hello, Toba. I am the Mysterious Bandit. You probably have not heard of me. This is due to the fact that I am such an expert I have never been caught—until now, that is." He turns the apple, finds the meat, looks up to Toba and bites deep. "I am so cunning and so graceful that it is the next day, perhaps even two, before my victims realize I have stolen from them. By then, I am long gone. That is the invisible mark of the Mysterious Bandit." He bows at his own introduction.

His lighthearted gestures make Toba feel a little at ease, yet her fingers tearing at the moist leaves of the bush tell her that they would much rather be somewhere else. As he goes on about his accomplishments—"food, wallets, hats from off their fool heads"—she studies this mysterious bandit. She is entertained by this boy—or is he a man? His clothes, which do not fit him and could use a washing, are not stylish but are in good repair. His skin is smooth and freshly scrubbed even to a girlish blush. His hair is in need of scissors, but shines and plays with the light streaming through the trees.

"And you, uh, *Toba*," he muses over her name as if it were she who offered a false title. "What is it *you* do to earn your food?"

"I live with my parents," Toba hears herself apologize.

"You are not married yet?" he asks with the surprise of one of her old uncles. "Such a lovely woman without a husband, hmmm?" He ponders the final bite of the apple and in a moment has it swallowed and the core spinning high in the air.

"And you?" Toba asks, watching his eyes dance at the sight of the core's flight.

"Yes, yes, I am married." He turns a sad face to the ground. "Three children—more on the way. Hungry and crying and no shoes in the winter."

Toba also turns her face to the ground, ashamed, feeling as though she has insulted him. "I am sorry . . ."

"Is it your fault?" he asks, with a pitiful smile. "Is it mine? They are darling, each one of them—you should see. This is why I steal. To feed them. To ease their hunger pains, until their next meal . . . whenever that may come."

Toba does not know what to say. It could not be proper to tell him he is right to steal, yet hearing this story, she thinks maybe stealing is not as wrong as it seems. She steps to the side, away from the bush.

But just when she is about to come fully out, to perhaps say something she does not mean to soothe this suffering boy (yes, he is a boy—with a young, fragile heart!), he laughs harshly, his eyes flashing.

"No, I am not married! No—no—not yet—so far I am lucky. That's just another sad, boring story to make the girls' hearts weep." He spins, arms high.

As if he'd reached out and smacked her, Toba retreats behind the protection of the bush, scolding herself. (Now who is the young one with the fragile and foolish heart!) She must get away from this thief.

"So we are not married. Should I give you a chance? Tell me," he says, taking out a turnip from his pocket and shaking his head at the shrunken form. "What kind of wife would you be, Toba?"

"The kind who is married to an honest man!" She returns his slap.

"Oooh," he says, covering up his heart, faking a terrible pain and laughing at her.

"Maybe I should call for the police," Toba warns, hurt that he takes her so lightly.

"Maybe you *are* the police?" he says, with no question in his voice. "Maybe I will have to run away from you or be thrown in jail? Maybe I will have to kill you in order to save my poor, hungry children?" His laugh now takes a brutal tone. "All ten of them!"

"I am not the police," she tells him, with false strength.

"But you are blocking my path. And you followed me from the market. And you saw me steal—" he pauses from his list to stare at Toba with a look of great seriousness. "I don't know if I can trust you."

"I'm not blocking your path." Toba's voice betrays her with a tremor.

"Then come out from behind that bush. Come out. I will not steal you like a tart from the baker. Sweet as you are—and hard as I might try." He smiles a smile Toba cannot help but trust.

She moves sideways, slowly, testing, careful not to move one inch toward him.

"Ahhh, yes, there we are, yes," he hisses. "What are you ashamed of? You are not ugly. No, not at all. You should not be so selfish. Your beauty is a gift—something not even the Mysterious Bandit may steal."

Toba looks for a place to run. But she does not. A sudden move could anger him. And it is very possible that he could be dangerous. A thief, she knows he is. Who is to say he is not also a murderer?

"Why do you steal?" Toba asks, changing the subject from herself.

" '*Why do you steal?*' " he mimics, mean, in a piercing, rude voice. "And if I tell you, what good will come from it?" he answers, with a bored tone, as if he's been through this before. "Will you cure me of my evil ways? Will you scold me? Tell me that it is wrong and that I should not take what is not mine?"

Toba runs. She does not decide that this is the right time. Her legs haven't the patience to wait for her dizzy mind to find its way.

But it is no use. He, as she had feared, is quicker. He does not grab her, but steps before her, blocking her way. She moves left. He steps in front. She moves right, he moves left.

"You want to know why I steal? All right, I will tell you," he says, looking into Toba's worried face. "I steal because I am no good. Is this what you want to hear? I steal because I am lazy—but then this is only half true. As I have said, stealing is a taxing profession—more or less." He laughs at his joke. "I steal because how else would I meet a Toba?"

"You are not poor!" Toba lets him know she is not going to trust such a lie. "Those are not poor man's shoes." She points.

"A sharp eye, my policeman." He picks up his right

foot and brushes his shoe top on the back of his left pant leg. "But perhaps I stole this pair of shoes? Would you believe I removed these shoes from a man, not just as he walked, but while he was *dancing*!"

His smile—though she fights—charms a smile onto Toba's face.

"But enough of this game—of what I do and what you do. We are here. It does not matter. We met over food. It is a fact that food is the greatest love potion in the world. We will eat." With moves of a true dancer, he takes off his long coat, removes the fruit from his pockets and lays out the coat on the ground. "Here, we have a fine table and chairs." He sits.

Now is the time for her to run. By the time he gets up, puts all his stolen food back into the pockets and the coat on his back, she could be in the crowded market, safe.

Toba sits.

"I will not eat the food," she says. "It would make me as guilty as you."

"You are not insulting me, miss," he says, choosing a cake over the fruits and vegetables. "If you do not wish to eat, it is your business. I cannot force you. But if you do not eat, then you will at least talk. So, tell me, if you are not married, then you must be off to America."

Toba, just to wipe that knowing look off his face, almost lies, but her curiosity's grip is too strong.

"How did you know?"

"How else," he asks, brushing the dirt and lint from his pocket off another cake, "could such a jewel go uncherished?"

Toba takes the cake, or at least her hand does. Her mind continues to wonder how it is that this unusual person has her captive without chains.

"They say America is a better place than this," he says. "But I can tell you that there is not one thief in all of America who would share his rewards with a stranger."

Toba bites into the sweet, layered cake.

"I apologize for the lack of napkins. I did not know I would have company. In America, I am sure they have napkins on every tree. I imagine it is such a place." He points to her blouse. "I believe in such a place stains are against the law."

Toba gasps at the red jelly on her blouse. She licks her fingers, but only makes the stain worse as she rubs and nearly tears the material.

"Too late," he sighs. "It is set." She does not give up her efforts. "Well, soon enough you will learn that the past cannot be changed. I can tell you from experience. I have tried."

The sudden shift in his voice brings Toba's face up from her blouse. She finds a quizzical, thoughtful look in his eyes.

They laugh together.

"Teeth, stains and a laugh," he lists, impressed. "You are a charmer, Toba."

Knowing that she is blushing, Toba tries to hide her face. She lowers her head and bites into the cake.

"I have a theory," he says, shifting to his knees as if to address an important meeting. "Food that is stolen is enjoyed more." He speaks not to Toba, but to the trees, the sky. "Yes, I believe this with all my heart. Yet I realize it is not a fact." He stands and begins to pace, hands moving with great speed and power. "A man who works—whether he is an honest worker or a slack-footer—and receives regular pay, believes his few rubles are owed to him. So-and-so many hours, he figures, are worth so-and-so many coins. He takes this pay and spends it on food. This, again, is expected. And because of this routine, he does not enjoy the food. He does not realize how delicious a good bread is or how soothing a hot glass of tea can be. This is because he feels he has earned the meals, and so they are not a gift." He pauses, watching Toba's wide eyes and the easy way she goes at her pastry. "But then there is the thief. He does not know what he will be chewing on the next day—or if, in fact, there will be anything to chew on at all the next week! He has little choice as he picks through the wares others have purchased. And because of this, each meal is fresh—even stale cakes from the lousy baker of Leman Street." He laughs to himself.

"Yes, food that is stolen is always blessed with extra flavor. It must have something to do with the forbidden fruit of Eden. I bet the apple that Eve fed Adam was mighty tasty!" He pauses over another cake, strokes its crust and croons his prayer. "Sweet, sweet forbidden fruit."

Toba knows well of what this poet speaks. Those memories which she keeps most dear are of those times she has tasted such "forbidden fruit." Secrets she has overheard and then told, times she's run off where she knew she shouldn't have even thought of going.

"There was a woman . . ." Toba begins to tell a story she has long needed to tell, one for which she could never find the trusting ears. Now, for no other reason than it seems right, she has decided to give this story, this terrible truth to the ears of a thief. "We called her the Stranger from Dansk. It was only a year ago that she arrived in Lenchintz with that sewing machine." Toba pauses; her words, like colors, paint the picture for her eyes, vivid as a dream, only painfully real. "This machine was not a monster. And now I can see that she was not the demon I had believed. But such is the work of our visions to keep us blind to the truth. This machine—it could sew so expertly, so perfectly, that it made even beautiful fabric ugly. This is how I saw everything then."

"I understand," he says. But Toba does not hear.

"And because I was to go to America, my Momma and Papa paid to have me receive lessons on this machine. Every day I would sit before its coldness, its blackness, and she was always taking my hands to it." Toba stops.

Her hands are clenched in fists. If she were right before the machine again, she'd do just what she had done before.

"What did you do?" the thief now offers only innocence. There is no man in him at all. The crumbs on his smooth face show how young he really is. It is a comic yet sad sight.

"I destroyed it," Toba says, biting at each word. "I threw the machine to the floor over and over until it was broken—and could never be fixed."

There comes a heavy pause.

"And the woman?" His voice is high, worried.

"I never saw her again." Toba bows her head and nearly cries. She can hear his breath, shallow and harsh.

"I will never tell, Toba," he whispers, now close to her. "Never. Trust me."

The thief's hands, as if handling a precious gift, take Toba's face in the soft of their palms and gently lift. He brings his face to hers. And touches his warm mouth to Toba's.

When they part, after how long it is impossible to say, Toba sees not the man that had frightened her and threatened her life, not the worried boy hearing a terrible tale, but a soft blend. His eyes, wide and hopeful, his mouth easy and full, his hands quiet behind his back as if he is hiding something he has stolen.

Toba does not think about what she has done, or—if she were caught and forced to speak of it—what was done to her, just as she does not think about the Stranger from Dansk. She does not think about how she will explain this to her Momma and Papa. Or the possibility of not explaining it to them at all. She does not think about this being her first kiss. She does not think at all.

What she does is need: to feel his mouth on hers again, to feel his strength pressed onto her. It is without thought that she leans over and slowly tilts her head, letting the lids of her eyes grow heavy.

She smells the dirt on his clothes, the fruit on his breath, the foreign scent of what could only be dark and dangerous. She is brought to him. His arm folds over, around her.

"I was not always a thief," he moans. "I was a cart boy. I was not always a thief. Not always . . ."

His long hair is fine in Toba's hand. She strokes it, letting it run over the back of her wrist.

"My father was an honest man . . ."

"Shh . . . shhh," Toba hushes, rubbing his thin shoulders.

"I wanted to be a teacher. Children like me. It has always been so. But I can hardly read a word. What good is an empty-headed teacher?"

"Yes . . . yes. I know . . ." Toba sighs in harmony to his sad song. The trees and grass whisper, *Forever. This will be forever.*

But what will happen if the grass and trees are liars? What will happen when time dulls the sun's warmth and chills the night's air? What will happen if this is not forever?

Toba does not think of this, either. She has given up the pains of thought. After all, where will such thought take her? Wherever, it could not be as perfect a place as this. What she does is tighten her hold around her thief, jealous of the little air between them. She smells his sweet hair. She holds his head in her lap. And when he has fallen asleep, she will take his thieving hands in her own and kiss them gently, gratefully.

The Photograph Album

Toba's goodbyes are her own to do with as she wills. Each is weighed, valued and painful to part with. Already she has wasted some on useless nonsense. Goodbye to the cord which has held her wet clothing to the sun's bright heat and wind's gentle waves. Goodbye to her scarred chair at the dinner table. Goodbye to the people of Lenchintz, some for whom she never much cared.

"Careful," Toba tells herself as she takes another, perhaps her final, tour through town. But to be careful at such a time is more than difficult. She nods to her weakness and to whatever she passes.

Her memory is an album of photographs, neatly ordered and inscribed with captions. With each nod she fixes her mind on an object, person, even clouded thought, and it becomes another photograph to be mounted and married with words. Goodbye to the leash that hugs the Halbereyers' tree though their dog has long since run away. Goodbye to the odd-shaped stone which poorly protects the searching earthworm. Goodbye to the Kosowskis' well, where many have tossed needed coins.

Why should Toba warn herself to be careful? The answer is not so simple. It is because, if she doesn't become stingy or at least watchful, she will have said goodbye to everything large and small in Lenchintz: every crack in every roof, every wrinkle in every face, every dream, every misery, and all that is between. And once she has said goodbye to all this, well then where would that leave her?

"So there she is!" Mrs. Tendril calls, pointing just to the left of where Toba is standing. "Soon she will be far from us," she tells her sister, Mrs. Jenkins.

Toba changes her direction, but it is too late.

"Toba! Toba!" Mrs. Tendril sings out, her voice shrill with the politeness of old age.

Goodbye to Mrs. Tendril's voice, dangerous as a dentist's drill.

Toba turns and smiles a practiced smile aimed to let the sharp-eyed note that not only does she not want to be bothered, but she does not want to be smiling, either. Mrs. Tendril, of course, has no such obedient eyes—hers swim like lost fish behind the thick lenses of her eyeglasses.

"You will be leaving us soon. Tomorrow, I am right, no?"

Mrs. Tendril does not bother to pause for an answer, but nods yes to her own question. "You will not remember, of course, darling, but I fed you when you were not yet a thimble." This makes Mrs. Tendril laugh, squeaky and painful. Mrs. Jenkins smiles and shakes her head as though she has heard the joke before.

"Well then, darling, this is goodbye, then. Goodbye and be well."

Toba knows what is to follow. Just as she knows there is no escape. Mrs. Tendril steps close, unfolds her arm from her sister's, takes Toba by the shoulders and brings her close. There is the musty smell of cupboards. Even in this uncomfortable position, Toba makes an addition to her photograph album. The caption: *Goodbye to Mrs. Tendril, her breath of stained bowls and dishes.*

The thought makes the loud, sloppy kiss and lifeless hug bearable.

"You should be well, live long and happy in this land that steals from us our children," Mrs. Tendril says in her most shaking, painful voice, wiping a tear from her eye with the handkerchief always tight in her hand. "It would be a mitzvah to remember an old lady."

Hearing Toba's promise of a letter to the sisters, Menachem, the cobbler, looks up and nods. His large hands do not rest from the badly beaten sole they are healing. Another picture? Toba considers. This is, after all, a most common sight. Why should she bother to remember old Menachem, hunched over someone's old shoe as if what he is doing is a matter of great importance? A goodbye for Menachem the shoemaker? Well, yes, why not, fine. Toba strains not to show any concern. She does not want Menachem to see that she is staring at him. That would be cause for him to ask what it is she is doing, then how she is, and what of the family? Of course, there would have to be some news of her journey. No, Toba wants to capture just the simple way he is. Slowly, but not too slowly, she turns and focuses her eyes on the faded beard that travels long down the side of the man Momma has said "has given breath to the tongues of the most tired shoes."

Toba's mind makes the noise. It is the flash of the camera's powder. She winces at the blinding light. The picture is taken, the soft wood of her memory carved. Toba studies her photograph, and in it she is able to see something she has never before noticed, though clearly it has always been just this way. Menachem's boots—how shining, clean and well cared for they are. Well, this makes enough sense. He is, after all, a cobbler, Toba tells herself. Who would trust a dentist with rotten teeth, or a school teacher who could not spell?

Goodbye to Menachem the cobbler's shining, well-cared-for old boots.

"So, tell me, what is it a girl—a woman, yet—does on her final day in the land where she was born? Tell me." Toba is surprised by Laban Horten's quiet voice. She turns to see him carrying two plump chickens by their scratching feet. They flap now only once in a while, having most probably given up their hope that Laban will take pity and decide to have fish for his dinner. "Lenchintz must seem very small at such a time, I am sure. You, it makes sense, are most likely on America's shores by now. Though I could be wrong. Obviously, if you were so far, you could not be listening to my senseless wanderings. And, by the same token, I must believe that I would not now be standing here, chickens in both hands, talking to myself."

Since she has known him, Laban has been studying in the yeshiva to be a rabbi. He is thoughtful, and unsteady on his feet as a skittish colt. His ideas, though unusual, are always a delight to Toba. Laban does not disappoint her this last time.

"You perhaps know that this is perfectly natural—your feeling as though you have undergone your long voyage and have already arrived at your destination," he goes on, the chickens swinging from his active hands. "When one is about to embark on a great journey, one is bound to let his mind travel ahead of his feet. This was true, you should know, of Moses and our people when they left Egypt. I am certain it crossed their restless minds as they slept in the desert how nice and comfortable the straw beds of Canaan would be—only to wake and find their shirts filled with sand." He seriously ponders such a thought as Toba contains her laughter with little success. "So, it seems the only advice I can offer you, on the eve of your exodus, Toba, is to sleep far from the sand."

Goodbye to Laban, the yeshiva boy, his thoughts flying wild, chickens upside down in his hands.

Toba wanders through the busy part of the market, her ears drinking in the music of the shoppers' and sellers' haggling and dealing. She inhales the blending aromas of fruits, baked goods, fish, meats, expensive perfumes.

"Ahhhh!" the baker moans, sadly. "So here she is, my best customer. Though it is true she has always been a devil to please."

"*Your* favorite customer, *poo*!" spits the fish peddler's wife, making a foul face. "Why, just this week she has bought such fish from me—the best she picked from my crowded cart!"

Toba stops to inspect and admire their wares, as the two playfully argue and taunt each other with gestures and threats mean and comical. For them, a pleasant, "So, how goes it this summer day?" is answered with, "What is it that you mean by that?" which quickly turns into a battle over who is better this day, what day it is, whether it is day, evening, morning or a bad dream they are sharing.

"Anything one says is right, the other says is wrong." This is the two rubles of sense the basket weaver adds, not bothering to even look as they curse the lives of one another. "Once, though, I was here to witness the moment the two *agreed.*"

At such unlikely words, the fisherman's wife and the baker still their movements and silence their arguing—no longer whether Toba is whose finest customer, but what her first bite will be in the land of America.

"This is true, the two agreed," the basket weaver now repeats, loud, standing, drawing a crowd, knowing this is just what his slow business needs. "And what is it, do you think, that they finally agreed to agree upon?"

No one even dares to guess, for fear of starting a war between the two merchants—both leaning over to hear just what they were supposed to agree upon, and preparing to disagree once they know.

"They agreed—now mind you, this is after centuries of working side by side—the two agreed to, what else, disagree!"

Toba's mind takes one more photograph. It is of the fisherman's wife and the baker—now separated by the smiling basket weaver, whose story earned him a laugh but no sales.

Goodbye to the marketplace of Lenchintz—without argument, my favorite place in the world.

Goodbye to the scrawny cat forever stretching and chasing after the invisible. Goodbye to the boy with the rag around his jaw soothing his sick tooth. Goodbye to the rabbis with the heavy, worn books and beards like rugs. Goodbye to Simpson, the lopsided water carrier. Goodbye to the rows of flowers in Mrs. Kelmer's garden. Goodbye to Mr. Kelmer's horse, who eats the flowers. Goodbye to the fat women who gather to talk over the day's news. Goodbye to the bird frightened into flight by Toba's footfalls. Goodbye to the way the sun warms the back of Toba's neck as she walks back home this sad, wonderful day.

Goodbye to all of everything. It does not matter to whom or to what Toba gives her farewells. Goodbye to this road. Goodbye to the tracks left by a swift carriage. Goodbye to the prints of each of her steps. Goodbye to the dust that will cover them. Toba's mind's camera catches everything and everyone. She does not ask them to pose or to dress in a certain way, or to smile, frown or think a silly thought. She photographs them just the way they are. And from now on, they will never change. Her Poland will be with her forever. And her memory will protect each photograph, each letter of every caption. She promises to visit them often. To turn the pages slowly, read the words aloud. And they return the promise to bring back to her years from now, just what she had heard this day. She will remark, much the way the old do to her, which are her favorites. She will hear just the way so-and-so would talk, how he had the habit of phrasing thoughts. What the weather brought that season. She will tend to the edges of each photograph, careful that they should not become worn and frail and lose their life.

Goodbye to the smoke rising and unfolding from her house's chimney. Goodbye to the full, steamy scent of Momma's boiled flanken. Goodbye to the whispering moments just between light and dark of these evenings.

Toba offers her goodbyes to even those pieces she tenderly places in her small trunk. She does not stop saying goodbye as she steps from her house. She will not stop saying goodbye even as she rides the great ocean. For once she stops saying goodbye, then where will she be?

The Poem

That morning will bring frost. So traveling
back will go badly. The branches breaking on
birds—stiff-tailed and lost.
One more time our mad song will rise
from the breathless earth.

You will think of the sea mending herself
with skin and bones of fish and wooden boats. My
white dress waving from the mast. Our stitches
fighting to hold.

We are small animals in America.
We live in doorways, outside windows. Our minds

are fixed on a great store of the future. Our bodies
are worn from leaping.
Our tongues lap tender beef, drowning
in a soup of desire, thunder and your hairs
tangled like seaweed.

On my way I will practice my speech.
I will walk this new step. I will
cry loud and sweet of this fine heart
forever obeying.

Toba does not sign her poem. It does not matter whose name is on the paper. The poem is hers.

"You cannot be stolen," she whispers, searching each word, satisfied. The phrases speak to her, at her. She listens to their anger, their fear, their forced hope. Her responses come in deep, constant nods and soothing hands. "Yes, yes, poor thing, I know, I know," she hushes, wondering if this is right.

Who is she, after all, to make a face of pain and say she understands such sorrow, even if this sorrow is her own? Who is she, even, to try to heal the wound? The poem, her poem, Toba believes, once it is born, once it is written, has its own voice, tells its own tale, feels its own sadness. Like a child who has her momma's looks and way of speaking, but nevertheless is not her momma, this poem suffers much like Toba, but its pain is not Toba's pain. What they share is the gift of misery, and yet this misery is a gift that can be neither offered nor accepted. It is a sacred place to cherish and wade, as if sorrow were a pool, cool, dark and tranquil.

There are two knocks at Toba's door.

"You are all right?" Momma asks, her voice raw.

Toba takes the poem and smothers its voice beneath her pillow.

The door opens. A chill is followed by the wide, agile woman whose face is Toba's. "You are—" She does not finish her thought with words. Toba forces a smile which trembles into a pout.

One more time our mad song will rise.

"Mrs. Kelpermeyer—the one with the problem with the leg. I saw her this morning." Momma eases her weight onto the bed. Like an invisible embrace, the mattress gives and pulls Toba close. "She told me of her son—you remember—Martin."

Toba tortures the pencil with her fingernails.

"She has heard news from him—through his brother, Nathan. It seems her Martin is making a 'fortune.' This is what she tells me, 'a fortune.' He is a salesman for an insurance company. 'You give them money when you are alive and when you die they give your money back.' This is a business? Ach, who cares?" Momma shakes her head. "Martin Kelpermeyer, with the ears like open cupboard doors, is making a fortune in America. Go figure."

The pencil cracks.

"You should not hate us, Toba," Momma speaks at

the floor in a low, coarse voice. "We do not deserve that you should wish on us this pain."

The bed quivers.

"Papa tells me, 'Yetta, from three, now we are again alone.' "

Our stitches fighting to hold.

"To see our baby taken from us, it is a terrible thing. Ay, what can we do? We do what we do."

We are small animals in America.

"You work. You have a family. It is a blessing you do not question. Who is there to answer?"

Our minds are fixed on a great store of the future.

"Maybe a miracle will happen. You pray for a vision. But the wrinkles on your face, they do not lie. We are old."

Our bodies are worn from leaping.

"From us come our children. From us they go . . ."

Your hairs tangled like seaweed.

The weight is lifted from the bed. The door closes. Toba waits for the sounds to leave the room. But the sounds remain. They are ghosts. Sighing, moving, speaking words heard this night, words heard in the past and those which will be heard long after Toba is gone.

She waits, listening. Hours pass before the silence comes. It settles like evening over the day, easing her into her pool. Slowly Toba becomes wet again. From beneath the pillow she takes the poem.

The house is sleeping. Toba lets her blind feet lead

her down the stairs and out the front door. In the cold moon's light, she walks into the garden. On a piece of land that has not been planted—a piece she has crossed over how many times without a thought—Toba bends to her knees. The soil is hard and bruising. She digs. Her hands take from the ground, grabbing up fresh grass, slippery weeds, tearing roots, clawing stones; her fingers, like starving worms, eat at the stubborn dirt of Poland.

From a distance, the mourners begin their walk. Their cries blend low and high. Their black suits, black veils and bowed heads follow each other. They are a chain, squeaking, moaning, moving in the painful, slow steps of the mourner's dance.

Toba plants her poem. It is a seed which will grow into a breathing tree. From its branches fruit will come. Who will eat from this tree? Toba does not know. Just as they will not know who planted the seed.

The mourners' grief rises in waves. The casket is lowered into the grave.

Toba buries her poem. It is her anger. It is her fear. It is what she most loves. She places the wrinkled paper on a fine bed of stones and earth. Then, with a light spray, as if she were a passing rain, she lets a handful of dirt sift through her fingers, showering the words. When she is done, there is only a smooth rise, a small hill where before there was a rough, unworked patch.

Who will come to mourn the dead? Toba does not

know. Just as they will not know who is buried here. Perhaps Momma will notice this unusual hill and for a moment take her mind from her gardening to wonder. Or maybe a dog will dig it up only to be disappointed that it is not a meat bone.

Toba considers whether she should have written the poem to take on her journey. She could fold it into a nothing to keep always. She shakes her head, no. You must bury the dead. It is their right. They do not belong to the living any more.

The thought comes that she might one day return to Lenchintz, just like a heroine in a book. She will come rushing off the boat, her new dress trailing in the mud, and run to the place where, as a young and silly girl, she had buried a poem with such terrible seriousness that years later she cannot help but laugh. It could be possible that her children will visit where their mother was born. She would, of course, have told them the story of "The Poem." A tale to keep them still as she bathed them or to take their minds from the endless rain outside. Perhaps it will be her children who will find the poem and carry it back to America? It does not matter.

On my way I will practice my speech.

She did not write this poem for anyone to read. She does not have the need to share her sadness with those who pity her, envy her, understand her.

I will walk this new step.

The mourners turn from the grave. The long, unbroken chain of black winds and fades.

I will cry loud and sweet of this fine heart forever obeying.

Toba loses herself in the darkness. It is a healing loneliness. In such a place, the seed will grow into a new life and the dead will be eternally remembered.

The Girl on the Boat

On the boat, this great city weaving deeply, wandering like a drunk who is struggling with a road that is wide, straight and well lighted, Toba sees a strange sight. Really, what she sees is not so strange—this is what most any other passenger would think if Toba were to pull them aside and whisper, "Look." But Toba has not said so many words since she and her trunk boarded the *Kingsman*. And what is more, she does not have the need to ask, to tell, to explain to anyone else what is and what is not to her strange.

The strange sight is a girl. From where Toba stands, she looks to be no younger or older than Toba herself. And like Toba, she is—or seems to be—alone. She is not now, nor has she been, acting oddly, as Toba has seen others behave—whispering to themselves, softly stroking their baggage as if they were frightened children, laughing crazily at nothing. This girl has not done anything at all, really, and yet, since she first saw her, Toba has been this girl's shadow—not a difficult job, since the girl sits for hours at a time by the ship's pointed bow, staring out at the endless water and sky with a face that is as naked as either.

So what is so strange? That she is pretty, dressed in a simple, clean skirt and loosely fitting blouse? That the coat she wears is new and seems to have trouble holding on to her shoulders as if they were enemies forced to be in each other's company? That her face is pale, clear, with freckles that look much the way speckles do on robins' eggs? That her eyes match the eggs' blue? Or that her ways, her manners, are slow, yet sure, thoughtful, yet easy?

What *is* strange is that Toba should know all of this about a girl whom she has never before seen, with whom she has never shared a word or glance—Toba is certain that this girl has not even noticed her. What *is* strange is that Toba is able to close her eyes—in fact, does close her eyes—even in surroundings as threatening and unfamiliar as this overcrowded boat filled with harsh voices and people with the faces of those who are about to do something terrible or have something terrible done to them, and can see the girl, perfectly alone, looking straight at Toba with an expression that changes from pity to hope to envy.

What *is* strange is that Toba is mysteriously captured by this plain girl with freckles that now look like specks of red dirt, and at the same instant she is forced to a distance. After all, Toba has been called many things—"shy" is not one of them. If she pleases, she could step past those in front of her, around their hills of baggage, over their children and introduce herself. "Hello, fellow traveler. I do not know you. You do not know me. But soon we will be related. We will be Americans."

Yes, she could do such a thing, even extend her hand in a traditional show of faith, and—who knows?—if their conversation were to become intimate, she could wonder freely, "Yes, perhaps our children will one day play together in this new land, America."

All of this would be what one might expect from Toba. But on such a day, it is not fair to expect anything from her. She remains still, still as the girl, knowing she will not meet her, ever. But this again proves how strange the whole matter truly is.

In her bed, a second berth that is short, narrow and has a mattress which grabs Toba as if it were angry with her, Toba tries to rest. She listens to the constant waves and the louder roar of the people crying, moaning of their lost families, their empty homes, their fears, their mules, their miseries. For a boat that was said to offer hope, it is very real to Toba that many of these passengers who have saved, cheated and lied to get where they are, are not hopeful at all, are not looking forward, but are saddened, and only pray that the captain will turn his great wheel in the wrong direction and when they dock they will walk off not onto the shores of America, but back onto Poland's soft soil.

"So why do they come?" Toba asks her book, the voice that she had planned would keep her close company on this journey. But the book only offers words on a page. And now, for all the great admiration and respect that Toba has learned to have for such things, it is obvious that words only offer answers, reasons and certainty. All of which seem useless, wrong and nothing but lies in the damp light of the lantern swinging from a nail alongside Toba's berth.

She wonders what it is the girl is doing at this moment. Walking about, wandering lost in this sea of people, on this ocean of emptiness? Dreaming a full and colorful dream of familiar faces, gentle touches and old jokes? Perhaps she is still on the deck, remembering her family that she has left behind—or perhaps she has no family behind to leave.

"Not all are so fortunate to have a family to say goodbye to," were Papa's words last night. Such an odd thought, Toba considers, remembering his face, lighted, and his eyes so dark. A tear comes to her own eyes, not at the thought of her Papa's words or his blindness, but because now she is not just thinking of him, but "remembering" him. The difference is as deep and wide as this terrible, still ocean.

Quickly, Toba stops her tear from falling, and closes her eyes. Such thinking about "remembrance" and "thought" is small and meaningless, and will do her no good at all in the place where she is going. And she knows just where she is going. In her suitcase are clothes made to be worn in America. There are no secret compartments filled with hidden hopes of a misguided captain or sudden current taking hold of the boat and leading them backward.

No, the only backward Toba travels is in her mind, wondering if this girl has found someone to talk with. *She searched carefully and finally found one trustworthy face among all of them, and sat down beside it. They will not say much, this man and this girl. She would not be attracted to the talkative type, nor is she given to meaningless babble.*

Having settled on the fact that this girl would not even begin to look for another to be near, Toba finds herself unable to rest. Her mind, like a spoiled child, will not let her be. And like a mother who has tried everything—scolding, threats, punishment—and has had no success, she is led by the whining voice out of her berth, past the musty curtains, down the five sturdy steps onto the ship's bottom deck.

Her steps timid yet curious, Toba moves through narrow, dark hallways. There is much written on the walls, all in angry red, thick letters—looking like warnings.

Warnings that do not make sense to Toba because they are in another language. "English for Americans," Toba mutters, proving some point. "This makes perfect sense. They take everything from everyone. Their language from the English, their children from Poland."

As soon as Toba reaches the outside, nearly running up the winding stairs, she is again searching for the girl. The roars and cries of the people are calmed and stilled by the steady fall of darkness. And in a moment, what is red and yellow in the sky grows darker than Toba has ever known. The stars are far away, the moon is lost in the thick blanket of black. The crowd, as if obeying a commandment, at once moves down to settle into their beds, leaving only a few stragglers, some who have no beds, others continuing their moaning, clutching their belongings, leaving Toba more room to slowly, like a cat, hunt down the girl.

Is she a dream? A vision? Could she be an angel sent from God to guide her? Toba cannot answer her own questions, just as she cannot help but search through the sweaty passageways of the ship. Level below level, her fear is tamed only by her desire to find this person, this ghost, this demon with the face of a painting, who haunts her.

Following the maze of narrow corridors, empty but for a few restless cigarette and pipe smokers, and those who stand, arms folded around themselves, waiting, Toba continues her hunt. Often she has thought of the first night away, how it would be for her on the boat that would be slowly taking her from Poland. She has imagined meeting people, sharing dreams, laughing about who they are, what they will one day be—"A day not so long from now, if it will be God's will"—and how they are glad to be rid of that old rag, Poland. More than imagined, she has rehearsed, as if in a play, how she would respond to different kinds of questions asked by certain types of people, all strangers. "Yes, New York is where I will live with Bella." "Behind are my Momma, Papa, sister, two nieces and their father." But in all her preparations, never did she imagine herself restless, in the middle of the night—the sound of the great ocean filling her head as the crowded boat carries her further and further—searching for a girl she does not know, with whom she has never spoken.

Is it that she reminds Toba of herself? This is impossible. Except for their age and the fact that they are both alone, they are nothing alike. Does Toba want to be like her? Why, she does not even know what this girl is like. The questions go on, inward, deeper, leading Toba finally, exhausted, to her bed, five steps up, behind the smelly curtain where her book with all the words and the answers sleep on her damp and lifeless pillow.

And when she wakes, her mind too clear, her body sore from its battles with the mattress, she aches not for food but for what?—she only half knows. Toba quickly dresses, and again begins her search. Through every corridor, on every level, checking each room, climbing ladders to pull aside curtains, disturbing sleepers, Toba prowls after the girl. She is someone Toba needs more than she needs her past, her family—for they are back across the ocean, in a place she can no longer touch.

So Toba runs on, as she would after a thief—though this girl has taken nothing from her; as she would to do an errand for her Papa—though she does not know what the girl wants from her; as she would to pick up her fallen nieces—though what relation could there possibly be between her and the girl? As she runs, the ship steadily makes its course, bringing her closer and closer to her destination. And when Toba does find her, when she sees the face she has seen everywhere but in front of her, it is as if the girl has been waiting all along for Toba to arrive. Posed, she stands on the bow of the boat, looking like a statue Toba has seen in paintings. She is leaning far out, dangerously close to the edge, but unafraid, as though she had promised herself, or perhaps someone who was unable to make the journey with her, that she would be the first to breathe the air of America.

Toba stops. She feels the slow rise of a feeling that can be given no name. She moves to the rocking of the boat, now finally at peace with its awkward rhythm. She does not move toward or away from the girl, and though the girl does not look at her, it is through the girl's eyes that Toba can see over the water spreading out all around them, over the sky, past the clouds and night's fading stars. It is a sight of not night, not day, not America and not Poland. There is no wind or even stinging spray of salt air. It is a moment unlike any she has ever before lived, a moment that shows Toba what she has been long searching for, searching for even before she boarded this boat. The girl's face offers a blankness. It is the blankness of an uncarved sculpture. Without thinking, by using the sensitive, precise knife of her imagination, Toba quickly strokes and carves in her own face.

When she is done with the fine lines beneath the eyes, the wave in the hair, Toba can place this new face anywhere. It is a face that belongs to a person who could be anyone. Anyone Toba wants her to be. It is the face of possibility. The face of the future. The face of a girl on a boat now more in America than Poland.

There are thousands of questions humming like bees inside Toba's head. She does not bother to swat them away or even think of quieting them with answers. To look the future in the face is enough.

Now it would be easy to go over and introduce herself, but somehow she feels this is of no use. She knows all she needs to know about the girl.

Toba stands still, still as the girl, letting the ship do all their moving, letting the blind ocean be their guide, letting the sea of people rise from their beds, climb onto the deck and fill the air, the world, with their song of moans, their faces of horror. To her own song Toba dances, eases into her own body, the slow motion of her life taking her, carrying her, freeing her, when a harsh voice shouts into her ear in a language coarse and foreign, "Better watch out for yourself, missy."